Mrs. Coverlet's Magicians

Mary Nash

HYPERION

NEW YORK

Text © 1961 by Mary Nash
First published by Little, Brown & Co. © 1961.
Reprinted by permission of Little, Brown & Co.

Volo and the Volo colophon are trademarks of
Disney Enterprises, Inc.

First Volo edition, 2001
1 3 5 7 9 10 8 6 4 2

The text for this book is set in 13-point Deepdene.

ISBN 0-7868-1518-3 (special promotion pbk.)
ISBN 0-7868-1517-5 (pbk.)

Library of Congress Catalog Card Number 00-63382

Visit www.volobooks.com

RS. COVERLET, the Persevers' white-haired housekeeper, set down a savory roast before the three children for supper. "Wild horses will never drag me away from you again!" she declared, plumping into a kitchen chair and beginning to carve fiercely.

"How about wild tigers?" queried the Toad, who was only six, and constantly said ridiculous things which mortified his older brother and sister. "Could *they* drag you away?"

"Wild tigers could not! Nor no other breed of wild beasts neither! Last summer was a lesson to me. I'll not be budged from my duty again! Not by ten thousand bloodthirsty savages with spears twenty feet long!"

"Suppose the savages tied ropes to their spears and harpooned you? Could *that* budge you from your duty?" The Toad leaned eagerly across the table.

"Never!" their plump housekeeper replied without a second's hesitation. "And take your elbows off the table!"

The youngest Persever gazed at his dear housekeeper with awe. If Mrs. Coverlet said a thing, it was true. In his mind's eye he saw the ten thousand savages, dressed in nothing but a few feathers, gnashing their teeth in despair, their spears all bent and their ropes in shreds.

The two older Persevers, Malcolm and Molly, who were thirteen and ten, were paying no attention to Mrs. Coverlet's extravagant talk. She had rambled on like this many times since her return last September from an emergency visit to her sick daughter, Marygold. It was then she had discovered that her three charges had not gone to stay with neighbors during her absence as they had been expected to do, but had continued living in their own house the whole time, completely on their own, enjoying a diet of hamburgers and chocolate ice cream, and having many interesting adventures. And although this had happened months ago, and it was now almost the end of November, Mrs. Coverlet had not yet fully recovered from the shock.

"Things weren't all *that* bad while you were away!" practical Molly couldn't help pointing out. It annoyed her that Mrs. Coverlet never seemed to be impressed by all the profitable, independent things she and her brothers had accomplished on their own: the fortune they had made selling their genuine tortoise-shell cat to Mrs. Dextrose-Chesapeake, the rich lady from New York, for instance. All Mrs. Coverlet remembered about last summer was the few careless oversights the children had made in their housekeeping.

"Things weren't *bad*, you say?" Mrs.

Coverlet glared at Molly. "To the day I die, I shall never forget opening the front door! Dust everywhere! Heaps of moldering socks! And my kitchen!" She put her hands over her eyes as if to shut out the sight. "On the floor under this very table, crumbs, and filth—and crawling there among them—swarms of—oh, I can't say it!"

"Are you speaking of my pet ants?" inquired the Toad, genuinely flattered at this dramatic description.

"I'm sure there weren't *swarms* of ants," Malcolm soothed Mrs. Coverlet. "Possibly five or six."

"And we certainly never encouraged them in any way!" said Molly, in an offended tone. "They used to drop in at mealtime to see what had fallen under the Toad's chair. It wasn't our fault if they did. And besides, those scraps would have been wasted if the ants hadn't wanted them. My goodness, Mrs. Coverlet, the Toad's cats sit under his chair to catch what he spills, and you don't mind *them*!"

It was true that at that very moment, under the youngest Persever's place, sat his six cats, Heather and her five kittens, their faces turned up for the morsels that were sure to fall.

"I'll not argue with you, Molly Persever!" Mrs. Coverlet said haughtily. "Only now that your dear father has been called away on business again and left me in charge, things will be altogether different!" Mr. Persever, the children's father, was a vitamin salesman for Bouncer's Drug Company. Recently he had inherited a tin mine in New Zealand, and this was the second time he had had to leave his family to take care of problems there.

"You're right, Mrs. Coverlet!" Malcolm assured her. "This time will be entirely different! We're in school for one thing. We haven't time to get into—to think up—uh—projects. And we don't need to earn money like we did last summer, because we have all that money we made then, still in the bank."

Mrs. Coverlet was never out of sorts for

long. When the plates had been cleared away, she put a blue baking dish on the table. "Dessert," she told them, a little apologetically. "I hope it ain't *too* bad!

The Toad jiggled up and down in his chair in anticipation. "*I* know what it is!" he informed them.

Mrs. Coverlet helped each Persever to something which strongly resembled her regular Friday-night leftover bread pudding, except that there were curious brown blobs all through it. While the older children regarded their portions doubtfully, the Toad poured cream over his, and shoveled away, muttering, "Yup, yup! Great! Didn't I tell you, Mrs. Coverlet?"

And then Malcolm was saying, "Why, Mrs. Coverlet, it's *good*!"

And Molly exclaimed, "It *is* bread pudding, isn't it? Only—"

"To tell you the truth," Mrs. Coverlet confessed, "it was an accident."

"I did it!" the Toad announced smugly, holding out his dish for more.

"That's right." Their housekeeper nodded. "He did. This afternoon while I was soaking my stale bread in milk for the usual Friday-night pudding, little Theobold came home from school. He climbed on a chair beside me to rummage in the cupboard for a snack, and first thing I knew, a package of chocolate chips fell right in my mixing bowl."

"The whole package!" agreed the Toad, smirking modestly.

"At first I tried to fish all the little things out, but—but I said, 'Leave them in, Mrs. Coverlet! It *can't* make your bread pudding taste worse, and it might make it better.'"

"I must admit," Malcolm said, passing his dish for more, "that I've never cared *too* much for stale bread pudding. But this is different!"

"The globs of chocolate melt," Molly mused, holding up a spoonful. "But they're still crunchy in the middle!"

"Best dessert you've ever made!" Malcolm summed up when supper was over.

"Let's have it every Friday night!" suggested Molly.

"Bless your hearts!" Mrs. Coverlet blushed, looking gratified. "Now go read to your little brother, Molly, and keep him out of mischief while I clean up."

"What shall I read you, Toad?" asked Molly. She had bravely undertaken to civilize her little brother, by reading aloud to him from the children's classics. Both she and Malcolm took the job of raising the Toad very seriously, since they had no mother. But trying to clear a path through the tangled jungle of his brain was the hardest thing Molly had ever attempted, and a less strong-minded girl would have given it up.

"Wanna hear 'Snow White and the Seventh Divorce,'" the Toad announced as he and Molly left the room.

"Saints help us! What is the girl reading to

the innocent babe?" exclaimed Mrs. Coverlet, staring after them.

"Du-*warfs*, Mrs. Coverlet," Malcolm pronounced patiently.

"Divorce. Just what I *thought* she said."

Malcolm shrugged his shoulders resignedly, and reached for the blue baking dish to see if there might still be a scrap of chocolate stale bread pudding clinging to the side. "Calm yourself, Mrs. Coverlet," he urged. "It's a very uplifting story. I read it myself as a child."

CHAPTER TWO

N O SOONER HAD Mrs. Coverlet set her kitchen to rights than she bustled into the living room where Molly was finishing the Toad's bedtime story and led him off to bed. And a moment later, Malcolm and Molly could hear his angry roars overhead as Mrs. Coverlet scrubbed him all over with soap and water.

Malcolm, who was staring out the front window into the night, gave a loud sigh and asked, "Where do you suppose Dad is, at this minute?"

His sister looked up at him. "Sitting on a plane, flying over the Pacific Ocean, as you perfectly well know! Why do you always make things so dramatic? We managed just fine last summer when he was away."

"It seems different this time," the oldest Persever continued in a dreary voice. "It was summer vacation then—warm out—no school—everything easy. Now it's winter, and Christmas is coming on."

"Not for almost a month, Malcolm! Anyway, what are you worried about Christmas for? Dad will be back by then."

"Call it a premonition," Malcolm muttered with a gloomy smile. "It's easy for you to be calm. You don't have the responsibility of two younger ones."

"Since when have I ever been a responsibility to you, Malcolm Persever?" It was a good question, for Molly was the sort of girl who was never late, never lost anything, never forgot anything, and tended to her affairs so efficiently that she had hours and hours left every day to manage the rest of the family's business too, whether anyone asked for her help or not.

There was a rather cool silence in the living room. Molly picked up the evening paper and began to read. All at once she burst out. "Will you listen to this, Malcolm!" and she read aloud. "'White Blizzard Flour Company announces its Tenth Annual Grand Baking Contest! Twenty thousand dollars in glorious prizes! First Prize, ten thousand dollars, plus full-length mink coat! Second Prize, white convertible car! Third Prize, electric stove with twin ovens! And for each of the hundred finalists, a set of the Encyclopedia Britannica!' And Malcolm, all you need to do is submit your favorite recipe!"

"I'm surprised you're planning to enter," remarked her brother sarcastically. "You are the worst cook in the family."

"You needn't be nasty," Molly said. "I was naturally thinking of Mrs. Coverlet."

"Are you crazy? Just because we like her cooking doesn't mean she could win a contest. She's not a chef, you know!"

"Listen to what it says about that: 'We are not looking for elaborate pastry recipes, but new, simple, imaginative baking ideas for today's busy and thriftwise homemaker.'"

"I still don't see what—"

"—Chocolate stale bread pudding!" Molly exclaimed rapturously. "It's certainly thrifty, and simple. And it couldn't be newer! It was only invented this afternoon!"

"That wasn't a recipe. It was an accident! The Toad was messing around in the cupboard over where she was working and—"

"—But accidents are exactly how things are discovered! Take Columbus! Take penicillin!"

"Save your breath, Molly. She'll never send it in."

"She doesn't need to!" returned his sister sweetly, tearing out the part of the newspaper with the notice about the contest. "I will submit the entry myself in her name."

Malcolm gasped. "You *can't*! It isn't honest!"

"Keep your conscience to yourself!" Molly retorted. "Mine doesn't bother me a bit!"

Malcolm shrugged. "What does it matter, anyway? She hasn't a chance. There'll be thousands of contestants."

"You don't think I'm such a fool as to count on the ten thousand dollars and the mink coat, do you? And I don't believe Mrs. Coverlet would have any use for a white convertible. But we have a perfectly good chance to win the encyclopedias, or even the stove."

"But we already have a stove and a set of encyclopedias!"

Molly waved this off. "*This* stove has two ovens," she reminded him. "And you can't have too many encyclopedias in a well-ordered home."

Malcolm blinked. He had thought of no reply to Molly's logic, when they heard Mrs. Coverlet coming wearily down the stairs.

When she appeared in the doorway, they saw that the front of her dress was soaked with water, her white hair was falling over her eyes, while her eyeglasses rested lopsided across her nose. One button was missing from her dress.

"He gave you a hard time, I see," Malcolm murmured sympathetically.

"Not at all," Mrs. Coverlet replied. "Just his sweet high spirits." She would never hear a word against the Toad. "He's tucked into his bed at last—the precious, innocent lamb!" She sank heavily in a chair.

"What's that you've got under your arm, Mrs. Coverlet?" asked Molly. Alas, there was very little which that girl's bright eyes missed!

Mrs. Coverlet reluctantly drew forth a luridly colored, tattered magazine. "I found it under his pillow," she admitted. "I was going to throw it out."

"A HORROR COMIC!" Malcolm shuddered. "And he knows Dad has forbidden us to buy them!"

"He told me he didn't buy it!" Mrs. Coverlet put in, rising to the defense of the wicked child. "He found it blowing around in an alley on his way home from school."

"I shall burn it at once!" Malcolm thundered, gingerly picking the grimy object from Mrs. Coverlet's lap. And as he carried it to the fireplace, this noble boy with the iron conscience turned away his eyes so that all he saw was the magazine's title, *Grisly Comics*, and the name of the first story, written in jiggly, magenta letters, "The Case of the Crawling Night Creature."

"Wait a sec, Malcolm!" Molly exclaimed, jumping up and reaching for the magazine.

"Now, Molly—" Malcolm warned her, standing on tiptoe and holding it away from her at arm's length for her own good.

"Don't be silly! I'm not going to read it," she said, snatching it anyway. "I just want to see— ah *ha!* I was right! He's cut something off the back page, and that means he's sent in for something! Now I wonder what!"

Sure enough, on the back cover of the horror

comic, among the advertisements for muscle-building systems, bicycles, watches, rings with secret compartments, easy ways to make money at home, and cures for warts and baldness, was a neat square window through the paper where something had been cut out!

"I dare say he found it that way in the alley," protested Mrs. Coverlet.

"Umm—maybe," Molly conceded. "But I think we'd better watch the mail. There's no telling what he may have sent in for."

Malcolm dropped the forbidden magazine into the fireplace and set a match to it. Mrs. Coverlet sighed, reached up to tuck in the loose strands of her hair, and watched the comic book burn. But Molly, who had another important matter on her mind, went out to the front hall, tore a piece of paper from the telephone pad, found a pencil, and then came and sat in a chair next to their housekeeper.

"Mrs. Coverlet," she began in sweetest tones, "all the time you were upstairs with the

Toad, Malcolm and I were talking about that delicious dessert tonight. Would you mind just *awfully* telling me exactly how you made it?"

"Why, it's my regular bread pudding—all but the chocolate chips."

"Couldn't you start at the very beginning and tell me, step by step?"

Mrs. Coverlet looked puzzled. "Why, Molly girl! What have you got that paper and pencil for? You're surely not going to take down every word I say! You're the last one I'd expect to take such an interest in cooking!"

"She has her reasons, never fear!" Malcolm muttered, getting up off his knees from the hearth and returning to his place at the window, where he stood with his back disapprovingly to his sister.

"Don't pay any attention to him!" snapped Molly, tossing her yellow hair. "He thinks just because the chocolate chips fell in by mistake it isn't a real recipe. But *I* say it's a genuine discovery and ought to be written down so it won't be lost to the world."

"Bless you, darling," Mrs. Coverlet said. "If it will set your mind to peace, I'll do my best." She squinted her eyes and puckered her mouth so that she looked fierce and worried, which was a sure sign she was thinking. "It's not easy to tell you how to make stale bread pudding, for you do it different each time, according to what you may find in your bread box."

"In that case," Molly suggested, "just tell me how you did it today."

"Well, there was three hot dog buns left from Tuesday night. I shaved the crusts off them, of course."

"Three—stale—hot dog—buns—crusts removed," Molly repeated slowly as she wrote.

"And a half dozen odd slices of dry bread."

"Six slices of dry bread."

"Oh, and there was two corn muffins from breakfast, I believe."

"—Got that," Molly nodded, after a moment.

"And when they were all together in my bowl, I poured my scalded milk over."

"How much of it?"

"Dear now, let me see! I always use my enamel pan, so it would be anyway a pint."

"One pint—scalded—milk."

"And, of course, you require your eggs, a couple of them, beaten a bit."

"Two—slightly beaten—eggs."

"And a half cup of sugar."

"One-half cup—gran—u—lated—sugar."

"How elegant it sounds the way you write it down!" Mrs. Coverlet exclaimed admiringly.

"And was it then that the chocolate chips fell in?" Molly asked.

"It was."

"A whole package?"

"Indeed. Except for a few bits that went on the floor which your brother jumped down and ate."

"One envelope—chocolate chips—full, or—as nearly so—as possible," Molly wrote accurately.

"And that was when I tried to fish them out, and little Theobold said leave them be, so I set the whole thing in my baking dish as it was."

"And how long did you cook it?"

"Mercy, I've not the least idea! I just kept popping a look at it now and then, and pressing the crust with one finger till it was brown and set right."

"Bake in—moderate oven—till firm and—golden brown. Remove and serve—piping hot—with fresh—cream."

"Listen to the girl!" Mrs. Coverlet cried, clapping her hands in delight. "If she doesn't take the *prize!*"

At the word "prize," Malcolm groaned from the window.

But Molly threw her arms around their housekeeper's neck. "Oh no, Mrs. Coverlet!" she said, "it's *you* who might take the prize—if you only knew!"

CHAPTER THREE

HE PERSEVERS' HOUSE was on a quiet street in the town of Loganbury. Across from them, and nestled behind a high laurel hedge, lived the Reverend Forthright, a bachelor and great friend of the Persever family. The outside of his house was covered with vines, and, inside, it was cluttered and comfortable. On the right of the Persevers', with no hedge, alas, between, lived Miss Eva Penalty. There was no vine growing on her white house. It was painted too often for ivy to get a grip.

Miss Eva's house was three stories tall, with glittering windows she was forever polishing. The Persever children, on their many goings and comings up their front walk, were apt to see Miss Penalty behind some pane or another, a white cloth in her hand, watching them with her weak, blinking eyes. The Reverend Forthright had often explained that Miss Eva's interest in them was purely friendly, but the Persever children had never learned to feel at ease with her. She was as thin as a bird, with a chin like a beak that jutted out hungrily whenever she asked them questions. Fond as she was of the whole family, she particularly doted upon the Toad. I am sorry to say that this rude little boy turned purple at the mention of her name and shuddered from head to toe as if he had swallowed a live bumblebee.

All the first week of December, out of her terribly clean windows, Miss Eva Penalty had been observing the Toad steal out of his house before school every morning and run down to the mailbox. And every morning she saw him come back empty-handed, until one day, as he reached in his hand, a grin broke over his face, and he scurried indoors with a small brown package concealed under his arm.

Miss Eva was so curious that later that morning she dropped in next door to have a cup of coffee with her friend, Mrs. Coverlet, and see if she could discover what the Toad had received in the mail. Unfortunately, she found the housekeeper in such a state of confusion and excitement that she never had a chance to bring up the matter. For the Toad was not the only person who received something unusual in the mail that day. After she had gotten the children off to school, Mrs. Coverlet had gone out, as usual, to see if there was a letter from Marygold, and found, addressed to her, an air mail letter from the White Blizzard Flour Company, with news so unbelievable that the poor soul scarcely knew which way to turn.

That afternoon, as Malcolm rounded the corner on his way home from school, he saw his friend

Reverend Forthright standing in the opening of his laurel hedge. "Over here, Malcolm!" he waved. "Been looking for you! I've got the kettle on inside."

When Malcolm reached his friend's side, the minister exclaimed, "What a time we've had with Mrs. Coverlet while you three were at school! How *do* you children dream up these schemes?"

"What schemes? What's happened? Is Mrs. Coverlet all right?"

"As well as can be expected, under the circumstances. Come on in." Mr. Forthright led the way through the cozy front rooms of his house till they reached the kitchen. "Good, you're boiling, I see," he remarked approvingly to his little teakettle. "Now, my boy, sit right there at the table. That's your cup on the left. Cream and sugar beside you."

"Oh, sir! What in the world has hap—"

"—Calm yourself, Malcolm! She's bearing up. Though it was a shock, as you children

should have considered in the first place, when
you did it secretly."

"But I still don't—"

"—The question is, what shall we eat with
our tea?" Mr. Forthright said, peering thoughtfully into his bread box. "Oh! Banana nut bread!
Courtesy of Mrs. Vault. We'll toast it." (Mr.
Forthright's lady parishioners took good care of
their unmarried minister, and kept him supplied
with cakes and bread, pies and casseroles,
which they slipped inside his back screen porch
and left there.)

"Yes," continued the Reverend Forthright,
sitting down opposite Malcolm. "All things
considered, Mrs. Coverlet is holding up well."
He dropped two slices of banana nut bread into
the toaster. "Of course, one moment she's laughing and saying she *must* go. Because it's her
chance of a lifetime to make a nest egg for her
old age. The next minute she's saying wild
beasts couldn't drag her away from her mother-
less babes! Why, oh, why did this have to

happen while your father's away?"

"But what *has* happened?" Malcolm burst out in despair.

"Oh, *come* now, Malcolm," said the minister reproachfully. "The letter from the White Blizzard Flour Company, of course! Inviting Mrs. Coverlet to the elimination Bake-Off in New York City. Don't look so amazed! You children sent in the entry, after all. You must have been expecting this might happen. Never mind, I didn't ask you over here to lecture you! We know you meant well. You always do, bless your hearts! The point is, you're the oldest, and you and I have got to put our heads together and figure out what to do."

"Bake-Off—Bake-Off," Malcolm was muttering to himself, trying to remember what Molly had read aloud to him about the contest that evening almost two weeks ago. He had hardly thought of it again. "There was something about a mink coat, and a set of encyclopedias, but I don't remember any mention of a Bake-Off, whatever that is."

"Oh, there's always a Bake-Off in these things," Mr. Forthright declared knowingly. "For the finalists. How else could they pick the top three winners? Have another slice, Malcolm. Careful, it's hot. Yes, it's in an enormous hall. Rows and rows of gleaming white stoves, just alike, for all the contestants. And there are reporters, and photographers, and home economists watching. And all the finalists cook their special recipes and the judges taste." Mr. Forthright licked his lips appreciatively. "It's a big thing, my boy."

Malcolm put his arms on the table, and buried his face in them. "I blame myself," he mumbled. "I should have read all the contest rules myself before I let her—"

"—For pity's sake, don't get your conscience all worked up!" Mr. Forthright begged, leaning across to pat Malcolm's shoulder. "Nobody's angry at you children. Actually, Mrs. Coverlet is terribly touched that you think that highly of her cooking. She never would have entered a contest herself. Today will always be a high point in her life, even if she can't go to New York."

"But she's *got* to go!" Malcolm burst out, looking up. "After all this, it would be cruel if she couldn't! It would be just for a day or two. We can manage."

Mr. Forthright looked grave. "There's the catch. The finalists have to stay a week. There's a whole floor of one of the big hotels reserved for them. And they have banquets, and public appearances and interviews with the press."

"A week's not so long."

"Oh, *but*," said Mr. Forthright, "if she wins the *grand* prize, she will be crowned Queen Snow Blizzard, and she has to stay in New York for three weeks of publicity. It was all there in the rules, you know. In the fine print at the bottom. The finalists have to agree to do it, if they accept the invitation to the Bake-Off. And let me make one thing clear, Malcolm. You three children are positively not going to stay alone in your house as you did last summer, and look after yourselves!"

Malcolm looked away.

"I only wish *I* could come over and stay with you," Mr. Forthright said regretfully. "But I'm leaving next week for a clergymen's convention in Boston and won't be back till Christmas Eve."

"This is the most terrible thing we've ever done to Mrs. Coverlet," said Malcolm. "We got her into this, and now there's no way for her to go."

"Wait a minute, Malcolm! There *is* a way. You children aren't going to like it, but for Mrs. Coverlet's sake you may be willing to make the sacrifice."

"What sort of sacrifice, Mr. Forthright?"

"There is a person who has kindly volunteered to stay with you until either your father or Mrs. Coverlet comes back. A single lady, with no family obligations. A close neighbor of yours. Good heavens, Malcolm! You're choking!

Take a sip of tea!" Mr. Forthright thumped him on the back.

When the fit had passed, Malcolm took a deep breath, drew himself up proudly, and assumed a tragic, older brother expression which would have infuriated Molly. "If having Miss Eva come over and stay is the only way, then we'll do it," he declared. "It'll be hard, but it's the least we can do for Mrs. Coverlet. There's one problem, though. I'm willing. And Molly will be." (She'd better be, he thought bitterly. She got us into this.) "But the *Toad*! You know how impossible he is. And how he feels about Miss Eva!"

Mr. Forthright nodded sympathetically as he escorted Malcolm to the door. "Talk it over privately among the three of you. You must all three of you be willing." He sighed. "And believe me, my heart goes out to you and Molly when you break the news to your brother."

CHAPTER FOUR

O ONE HEARD Malcolm let himself in the front door. He stood just inside for a few minutes, composing his thoughts and considering the most tactful way to discuss Miss Eva with the Toad. As he hesitated, his sister came round the corner from the living room. One look at her face told Malcolm she knew everything.

"I've been at Mr. Forthright's discussing it," he informed her.

"Well, the whole thing's my fault," said Molly in her straightforward way. "It seemed such a marvelous idea I was carried away. Me, of all people! With my common sense. Being so careless! I never read down to the bottom of the rules where it told about the finalists' having to go to New York."

"Never mind," her brother consoled her. "Your intentions were good. That's the main thing. We'll manage to get through living with Miss Eva, somehow."

"It's not you or me I'm worried about," Molly agreed. "It's you-know-who."

Malcolm nodded. "We must break it to him carefully. So he doesn't go into one of his purple rages."

"Break it to him? Don't you think he knows already? The minute he and I got home from school we knew something had happened. Mrs. Coverlet was running around in circles. We couldn't make out anything she said till she handed me the letter from the White Blizzard people. And then we all were so happy and laughing! The Toad was strutting around with his chest out, saying *he* ought to be going to New York because he invented Chocolate Stale Bread Delight. And just then Miss Eva came bursting in the back door. She'd seen us getting home from school, no doubt. Before the Toad knew what was happening she grabbed him in her arms and squeezed and hugged him, and said: 'My poor angel baby! I'm going to move right in and stay with you while Mrs. Coverlet's gone!'"

"And what did *he* do?" Malcolm gasped, listening in horror.

"He was so taken by surprise he couldn't do anything! She had him pinned in her grip. But I could see a little glimpse of his face over her shoulder. And I think he'd stopped breathing. The first chance he got, when she shifted her hold on him to start kissing the *other* side of his face, he ducked and tore upstairs, and he's been up there ever since."

Malcolm looked grim. "We've got to talk to him before he does something rash."

They hurried upstairs to the Toad's bedroom, where Malcolm knocked and, receiving no answer, tried the knob. The door was locked, and there was no sound within. "That's peculiar," remarked Malcolm. "You'd think he'd at least snarl at us."

"Better break in," Molly advised. "Here's a bobby pin. It's quite easy."

At this suggestion, honorable Malcolm looked pained, and asked his sister how on earth she had ever discovered such a sneaky thing as opening people's doors with bobby pins.

Molly interrupted him by poking him out of her way with an elbow and kneeling down before the door. "This is an emergency!" she snapped. "I haven't time to argue with your silly conscience." At that the bolt gave a click, and the knob turned.

The Toad's room was empty and bitterly cold. The window which looked out on the low roof over the front porch was wide open. Even the cheerful cat box, which was usually full of Heather and wriggling kittens, was unoccupied!

"Gone!" Malcolm groaned, sinking upon the Toad's bed.

"Lift up, Malcolm! A note!" Molly tweaked a scrap of paper from beneath her brother and read: "'Gon to New Yok to stay Mis Deskstroke Chesalpek and takun al my cats.'"

CHAPTER FIVE

O MRS. DEXTROSE-Chesapeake's! I might have known!" said Molly. Mrs. Dextrose-Chesapeake was a particular friend of the Toad's. They both loved cats, and he had met her the summer before when she bought his famous tortoiseshell, Nervous, from him for thirteen hundred dollars and gave him Heather and the five kittens in the bargain. The Toad had later visited her in New York, and been badly spoiled there. He had always had a high opinion of himself, but after his stay in the big city, the places he had been, and the things he had seen, he was even more difficult for Malcolm and Molly to manage.

"Well, don't just sit there, Malcolm!"

Molly scolded as her brother slumped on the Toad's bed, staring despairingly at the open window. "We've got to go after him!"

They tiptoed downstairs and lifted their jackets from the hooks in the hall closet. In the kitchen they could hear Mrs. Coverlet preparing supper.

The clock in the hall said five. "If we can get him back by six, she needn't ever know!" Malcolm breathed.

Outside it was a cold brown twilight. They could just make out the spidery outlines of three bicycles leaning against the wall of the garage.

"Good! He didn't take his bike!" Molly noted.

"I suppose he couldn't ride and carry six cats."

"Then I'm *sure* we'll catch up with him!" Down the shadowy street pedaled the two older Persevers, turning left at their corner, then right a few blocks farther along, and coming out upon the main highway to New York. As far ahead as they could see stretched the wide, empty road, and as they made their way along it, the November wind turned their knuckles blue, and their fingers white on the handlebars. At last, coming around a bend they made out a small familiar figure at the side of the road, with something that appeared to be a large sack slung over one shoulder.

The Toad took no notice of them as they stopped abreast of him and leaned over their handlebars to pant. He was shaking his fist and calling crossly in the direction of a tree growing on the bank beside the road. Malcolm laid down his bike and came and stood next to him. The lumpy white sack on the Toad's back turned out to be a pillowcase, which constantly heaved and bulged, and from which came the sound of irritated cats.

"Is one of them up that tree?" Malcolm asked kindly.

"None your bizness!" snarled his ungrateful

little brother, but then added in a worried tone, "It's John Napkin." John Napkin was Heather's one black kitten. He was the naughty one in the family, and he was the Toad's favorite.

"I'll get him for you, Toady." Malcolm strode up the steep bank and disappeared into the shadows, where they heard him crashing and grunting as he climbed the tree in the direction of an invisible meow.

The Toad gave a despondent sigh, shifted his heavy pillowcase, and clutching it tightly against his stomach so that nobody else could escape, he sat down wearily on a log by the side of the road. Molly got off her bike and came and sat beside him. Though she had had every intention of scolding him, all that came out when she opened her mouth was, "Toady, I'm *so* glad we found you!"

Her little brother did not reply. On the other hand, he did not move away from her as he could easily have done, since the log was a long one.

After a minute they heard Malcolm's

triumphant voice high in the air. "*Now* I've got you! Don't scratch, John! I'm only rescuing you!" Then there were grunts and the sound of crackling twigs as Malcolm came down; and John Napkin was presently redeposited in the pillowcase. A loud roaring purr inside it told them how glad Heather was to see her wandering child.

"Hear that?" Malcolm asked the Toad sternly. "You see, no matter how much trouble a child may be, its family is always glad to find it safe and sound! Now climb on the front of my bike and we'll go home!" The oldest Persever braced his bicycle while the Toad reluctantly got onto the handlebars. Molly held the pillowcase until he was settled and then handed it to him. It was a hard trip home. The Toad had to keep his balance with one hand while clutching the shifting pillowcase with the other. And there were several emergency stops while Molly jumped off her bike to retrieve kittens who escaped despite the Toad's efforts to keep them stuffed down.

It was dark when they reached their house and crept in the front door. To Malcolm's relief the clock in the hall said only ten minutes of six. "We made it before supper!" he whispered. "Upstairs, everybody!"

In the Toad's bedroom, with the door closed behind them, Malcolm and Molly sat down side by side on their younger brother's bed. The Toad, meanwhile, his face like a thundercloud, turned the pillowcase upside down and let Heather and her rumpled children tumble out.

"All right, Toad!" Malcolm said. "We want to talk to you." The Toad braced his feet, stuck out his lower jaw, and scowled defiantly.

"You realize that this chance of Mrs. Coverlet's to win ten thousand dollars is a once-in-a-lifetime opportunity, don't you?" Molly asked. "It would mean security in her old age." The hard-hearted Toad stared unfeelingly at the ceiling.

"If she ever suspected that you tried to run away rather than be left with Miss Eva, you know Mrs. Coverlet wouldn't have the heart to leave you," Malcolm added. The Toad gazed stonily at the wall.

"Mrs. Coverlet has taken care of you for six long years without once complaining—in spite of all the trouble you've caused her!" Molly reminded him. The cold-blooded Toad looked quite unmoved.

Malcolm turned solemnly to Molly. "Do you remember the time the Toad plugged up the drain in the cellar floor with rags and turned the water on down there overnight, hoping he'd have an indoor swimming pool by morning?"

"Indeed I do!" Molly sighed. "Mrs. Coverlet was mopping down there for three whole days!"

"And do you remember the time he took a bottle of maple syrup and a paintbrush and did one whole kitchen wall?" Malcolm asked.

"That was my flytrap!" sputtered their little brother. "I propped open the kitchen screen door, and thousands flew in and got stuck in the goo, and I was swatting like anything! I bet I could have gotten rid of every fly in Loganbury if you dumbheads had left me alone."

Malcolm did not even look at him. "Molly," he said in a somber voice, "do you remember the time he mislaid a garter snake in the house and forgot to mention it to anybody?"

At this the Toad winced and put his hands over his ears, but Malcolm went on relentlessly. "I'll never forget poor Mrs. Coverlet's scream when she put her foot in her bedroom slipper and something curled around her toes!"

"Stop! Stop!" howled the Toad, wrapping his arms around his head.

"She's always been so forgiving," mused Molly wonderingly.

"And to think," Malcolm said, "that at last, after all these years, we have a chance to repay her for what she's been through."

"Okay! Okay!" the Toad burst out. "I'll stick it out here with you guys and Miss Eva. Now let's drop the whole subject!"

"Promise?" Malcolm demanded, looking hard at him. "You won't try to run away again, no matter what?"

"Sacred word!" groaned the Toad.

Malcolm and Molly had barely exchanged a look of enormous relief when they heard Mrs. Coverlet calling them down to supper.

As soon as they were settled around the table, Malcolm cleared his throat and told their housekeeper, "We've talked it over, Mrs. Coverlet, and all three of us want you to go to the Bake-Off!"

Mrs. Coverlet's face cracked into a wide smile. "My darlings! Are you *sure*? Even you, Theobold? I won't stir if it makes you unhappy!"

The Toad was not listening. With his fork in the air and his mouth pulled to one side, he was wearing a crafty, preoccupied expression.

"Mrs. Coverlet is speaking to you, Toad," said Molly.

"What?" he muttered vaguely. "Oh, sure. It's okay if you go."

A terrible suspicion rose in Molly Persever's keen mind. It was true that the Toad had given them his sacred word not to run away again. All the same, she had the feeling that at this very moment, before her eyes, her unmanageable little brother was plotting some new way of escaping Miss Eva's visit. But of course, she comforted herself, the Toad was only a very young and foolish child, and no matter what he was up to, he was no match for herself and Malcolm.

CHAPTER SIX

I T WAS THE afternoon Mrs. Coverlet was leaving for New York. The Reverend Forthright was expected any minute now at the Persevers' house to take her to the airport. The three children, just home from school, were being helpful in every way they could think of.

Malcolm, for instance, was on his knees in the upstairs hall, trying to lock Mrs. Coverlet's suitcase with a key which Molly, breathing heavily over his shoulder, had warned him did *not* belong to it.

Sure enough, all at once the lock gave a click, became perfectly stiff, and the key was trapped in its jaw.

"See?" Molly exclaimed. "I told you not to force it! That's the key to the *brown* suitcase! Now how is Mrs. Coverlet going to open it tonight at the hotel, I'd like to know?"

While they were jiggling the key and talking in low voices, Miss Eva Penalty, humming and blinking her pale, damp eyes, shuttled between her house and the Persevers', bringing armloads of clothes, and last of all, a white enamel tray, clanking with brown medicine bottles.

"I do hope that isn't for the children!" Mrs. Coverlet murmured, coming to the door of her room just as the tray went by. "They're hardly ever sick, and when they are, they're holy terrors about taking medicine.

"I dare say I can persuade them," Miss Eva replied with a narrow smile, setting down the tray very carefully on a bathroom shelf.

Where was the Toad all this while? Why, making himself useful by—good heavens, the Toad was doing nothing whatever to help anyone! He was curled up on the porch hammock with John Napkin, holding that black kitten tightly and whispering into one twitching ear, that if it hadn't been for his jumping out of the pillowcase and getting up a tree and delaying them, they would all be at Mrs. Dextrose-Chesapeake's by now, leading a life of ease and pleasure—he, his mother Heather, and the rest of the family, Mary Mouse, George Soup, Ernest Waffle, and Sally Egg.*

A motor stopped in front of the Persevers' house. The Toad sat up in the hammock and looked over the porch railing. It was not Mr. Forthright's old blue car as he had expected, but the delivery truck of Mr. Romaine, the grocer. The Toad was a boy who was always interested in food. He put down John Napkin, jumped off the hammock, and ran down the porch steps.

*If you wonder why the Toad's five kittens had five last names, though they were brothers and sisters, all I can tell you is that when Molly asked him the same question, he told her disgustedly, "Those aren't their last names, dumbhead! They're their middle names. Their last name is Tickle."

Mr. Romaine had opened the back of his truck and was pulling out carton after bulging carton and setting them on the sidewalk. "Is all that for us?" asked the Toad admiringly, as he came close.

"Every bit! Miss Penalty called me and told me she'd be staying with you, and placed a large order." The grocer set down a box full of vegetables, some gray, some yellow, some speckled, some purple, some small, some as large as footballs, but all rolling and bumping against each other in an unsightly and revolting way.

"Help! What are *those* things?" the Toad exclaimed.

"Eggplant, squash, cauliflower, rutabaga, and okra."

"Oak *what*?"

"Okra, boy. Okra. A vegetable. Awfully good for you, though it's a little too—er—gooey for some." Mr. Romaine tried hard not to pucker down the corners of his mouth as he described it. "Miss Penalty is a great one for vegetables.

We don't get many calls for okra. Most people can't stand—uh—can't *understand* how to fix it."

"I don't suppose you'd know what she's giving us for supper tonight?" the Toad asked, taking his eyes off the vegetables and letting them roam hopefully over the top of the other cartons.

"Indeed I do!" replied Mr. Romaine. "Liver, beet salad, and stewed rhubarb for dessert."

The little boy's shaggy eyebrows descended over his brown eyes. His ears were growing a dangerous red. "Where's the stuff for afterschool snacks? I don't see any cookies, or peanut butter, or marshmallows, or *pop*, or *anything*!"

"Miss Penalty disapproves of sweets and eating between meals," said Mr. Romaine, taking the pencil from behind his ear and starting to check things off a long list. "Though she did order a pound of dried prunes for a treat."

"Dried *prunes*!" An ugly growl escaped from the Toad. Mr. Romaine looked up from his paper in astonishment. But at that moment Mr. Forthright's car drew up behind the grocery truck and gave a cheery honk. At once the front door of the Persevers' house opened, and out came Malcolm and Molly lugging Mrs. Coverlet's suitcase, followed by Mrs. Coverlet in her best clothes. The plump housekeeper was helped into the front seat, and the children and the suitcase stowed in back. Mr. Forthright leaned out of his car window and called politely to Miss Eva, who was watching them from the front porch, that there was plenty of room if she'd like to come. But Miss Eva said no, she'd take advantage of the quiet to "organize," and get the groceries put away.

As soon as they were under way, Molly turned to her little brother, who was sitting between herself and Malcolm, scowling hideously, and whispered, "What's eating you, Toad?"

"I'm going to take my cats and go live on an uninhibited island!"

"*Hab*ited," Molly corrected him primly.

Malcolm looked up from the suitcase on the

floor before him, where he had been sadly studying the key still jammed in the lock, and said, "Now let's have no funny business about your leaving again, Toad. You gave us your word."

"Yes, but you guys haven't seen the stuff she's going to make us eat!"

"It can't be that bad," Molly reproved him. "A few more boiled vegetables than we're used to, but it won't be for long."

"Don't be silly, Toad! We don't have to take medicine unless we're sick, and we're never sick."

"I am going to be *very, very* sick if I have to eat those terrible speckled vegetables, and that oak root, or whatever it is!" The Toad folded his short arms grimly. "Well, don't worry about my running away. I gave you my word. But don't blame me if I *take other steps.*"

"Other steps?" asked Molly. So he *was* planning something! "What kind of steps?"

The Toad shrugged. "Just steps. I don't say I will, and I don't say I won't. Only don't blame me if I should."

CHAPTER SEVEN

ELP YOURSELF TO a little more of this delicious beet salad," Miss Eva urged Malcolm at supper as she passed him a platter with a mound of purple nuggets, nestling on a lettuce bed.

"I'm pretty full, thank you," replied the oldest Persever. "Here, Molly. You look hungry. Why don't you have some?"

"Why, thank you, Malcolm, but I'm afraid I'm full too," Molly murmured sweetly, as she stepped hard on her big brother's foot under the table, and hastily handed the salad in the Toad's direction.

But when the plate made its sudden appearance under the Toad's nose, he made no effort to take it from Molly but simply stared at it in horror. I'm afraid the youngest Persever did not show the delicate manners of his older brother and sister.

"It's a good thing I brought over my large bottle of cod-liver oil tonic!" Miss Eva remarked, taking the salad plate and putting it down. "You'll all have some at breakfast tomorrow. Such miserable appetites! Ruined by sweets and constant eating between meals. Never fear, we'll have all that set right in a few days."

Under the Toad's chair sat his six cats, as they always did at mealtime so as to catch the tidbits which accidentally fell off his fork on the way between his plate and mouth. Tonight, Heather and her family were amazed at the feast which came their way; every time Miss Eva looked away, the Toad passed down another piece of liver to them until he had neatly disposed of his whole helping. The last morsel went to George Soup, the gentle gray kitten.

When John Napkin saw this, he began to pull it out of his brother's mouth, and George Soup set up a howl.

"What's that?" Miss Eva demanded, peering around the table in her nearsighted way.

"Somebody must have kicked one of my cats," the Toad suggested helpfully.

"Cats! Where? Under the table while we're eating! How disgusting!" Miss Eva jumped to her feet. "Scat!" she cried, leaning over and flicking her napkin at them. The cats hurried away upstairs to their box in the Toad's room.

"Excuse me, I don't want any dessert," said the Toad, slipping out of his chair. He knew in advance about the stewed rhubarb, from his talk with Mr. Romaine. He also remembered a certain candy bar he had put under his mattress some months ago in case of emergency.

When he had finished the candy bar, the Toad invited his cats to a game of grab-my-toe. They were willing to play, so the Toad jumped up and stood in the middle of his bed, while the cats took their places underneath it behind the skirt of the spread.

Then "Ready! Go!" shouted the Toad and began running the length of the mattress, back and forth, with great leaping strides, now and then hopping down onto the floor, first on this side, then on that, while the cats darted out their paws to catch his feet before he could get up safely on the bed again. The game was just reaching a wild and reckless pitch when the door opened and there stood Miss Eva! Catching sight of her, the Toad stopped short in the middle of a beautiful bounce, fell flat back on the bedspread, his hands to his sides, his eyes fixed on the ceiling, holding his breath so as not to pant, and trying to look like a boy who had been lying this way ever since supper, thinking deep thoughts. Under the bed the six cats, whom Miss Eva had not noticed, pulled in their paws and lay perfectly still.

"What is the meaning of this, Theobold?" demanded Miss Eva. "All this overheating and excitement before bed is dreadful for the system! Look at the state of these bedclothes! Get into your pajamas, and I will straighten things up and tuck you in all snug."

Snug was right. A few minutes later, after he had crawled between the covers, Miss Eva, working down one side of the bed and up the other, had tucked the blankets and sheets around him so tightly that his arms were pinned to his sides and he could scarcely draw a breath. Then, while he was trapped, she bent over and planted a loud kiss on his forehead.

All this time, under the bed, the kittens had been watching Miss Eva's shoes walking to and fro. They would have loved to box with them, but their mother, Heather, would not allow it. However, when Miss Eva leaned over the Toad to kiss him, and her two pointed toes suddenly poked under the spread right in John Napkin's face, he could not resist giving them a jab. Miss Eva jumped back. "Help! Something grabbed my foot!" She twitched up the spread and looked. "Aha! Those cats again! Out they go!"

"But they live here!" sputtered the Toad, helplessly trying to work himself loose from his covers.

"Animals should never be kept in a sleeping room! It's filthy and unhygienic!" Miss Eva declared. "I shall take them down to the basement." With that she fetched the cat box over to the side of the bed, and getting down on her knees she scooped out Heather and the five kittens and deposited them inside, all too taken by surprise to protest. "They will be perfectly comfortable in the furnace room," said Miss Eva, getting to her feet and marching to the door with the box. Over its sides, the cats looked down reproachfully at their friend, the Toad. They could not understand how he could lie there like a mummy and permit such a terrible thing to be done to them. At the doorway, Miss Eva balanced the box on one hip while she turned off the light and pulled the door closed. Then her steps went *plom, plom,* downstairs.

The instant he was alone, the infuriated Toad began to thrash about in the darkness like a harpooned porpoise. At last one arm came free, and with its help he was able to push away the covers and sit up. "My own cats!" he hissed fiercely. "That *does* it! My private property! My special present from Mrs. Dextrose-Chesapeake! Put in the *cellar*. Hah! That's the last straw! I'm taking steps!"

With that the little boy slipped out of bed and tiptoed across the room to his closet. He opened the door, groped about till he found his flashlight, turned it on, and closed the closet door on himself. By the faint light he rummaged among boxes and toys till he came to a square box marked "Alphabet Blocks."

"Here we are," he whispered, and sat down cross-legged on the closet floor with the box on his lap. When he took off its lid, there were no blocks inside but, instead, that small, mysterious brown package he had received a few days ago in the mail. So this is where the crafty child had hid it! His sister Molly would have given anything to know about the existence of this package. And if she had, many strange things which happened in the next weeks might never have happened at all, and life at the Persevers' would have been much more ordinary and not nearly so interesting.

The Toad unwrapped the brown package. There were only two things inside. He knew what they were because he had inspected the contents the day it arrived, before he hid it in his closet for future use. One was a little, crudely printed pamphlet with a dozen pages of writing and several more of diagrams and odd designs. The other was a blob of something gray and shapeless, resembling a lump of clay. "Hmm—" murmured the Toad, pricking up this curious object and turning and warming it in his hands. "Wonder what you use this for?"

He laid it down and opened the booklet to the title page, his forehead furrowed as he sounded out the unfamiliar words. "'A Do-It-

Yourself Book of Practical Witchcraft. Chapter One: How to Cast Charms and Spells.' Hm-m-m-nothing there I want. 'Chapter Two: Love Potions.' Oh, ugh! 'How to Use a Divining Rod.' Wonder what that is. 'Chapter Four: Weather Brewing: How to Make Rain, Hurricanes, Cyclones, and Blizzards.' Boy, oh, boy, oh *boy*! I'm going to try a few of those! 'Chapter Five: Hexes and Evil Eyes.' *Now* we're getting somewhere! 'How to Make Your Enemies Powerless.' That's it! That's what I want!" By the shadowy gleam of the flashlight, the little boy's face broke into a sly grin. "Wouldn't it be something, though, if this could really work!"

CHAPTER EIGHT

HAT'S FUNNY!" Molly remarked. It was eight o'clock next morning and she was standing in the kitchen doorway, looking inside.

"It isn't like Miss Eva to oversleep," Malcolm agreed, looking over his sister's head, then stepping past her. "She said she was going to get up at five this morning to boil gruel for our breakfast. Here's the pot where she was soaking it overnight." On the kitchen table sat a saucepan of cold water at the bottom of which lay some speckled bits of no-colored, uncooked porridge.

"Somebody ought to go upstairs and knock on her door," Molly said. "Maybe she's sick."

"She's not sick," a jaunty voice assured them, "but she won't be coming down." It was the Toad, standing at the top of the cellar steps with his cat box in his arms. The six rescued cats were purring loudly. The Toad looked wonderfully refreshed after a night's sleep, and very pleased with himself.

"She won't be coming down?" practical Molly demanded. "How do *you* know?"

"Because I know what I know," said the irritating child, complacently setting down the cat box in the middle of the kitchen floor. "Now you all wait right there and I'll get you your breakfast."

"I'm going up to see!" Molly turned on her heel and marched through the house and up the stairs.

"Come in-hin!" sang out Miss Eva's voice, when Molly knocked. She was sitting up in bed, propped on her pillows, sweetly smiling.

Molly Persever blinked.

"Isn't this the silliest thing?" Miss Eva giggled. "I suppose little Theobold told you. He must have had some sixth sense. On his way downstairs this morning he knocked and said he was just checking to see if I'd be coming down. Such a sensitive child!"

"I'm sorry you're not feeling well," said Molly sympathetically.

"But, my dear, I never felt better in my life! It's the strangest thing. My alarm went off at five, and of course I bounced out of bed as I always do, put on my wrapper, and started for the door. And then—I can't explain it—but I had this overpowering urge to crawl back under the covers and just *stay*! First morning in thirty years I haven't been up and busy by six! To tell the truth, Molly, I'm enjoying it so much, I don't know *when* I'll get up!"

"I see," said practical Molly. "In that case, I'd better bring you some breakfast on a tray before we leave for school."

"Oh, I'd *hoped* you'd say that!"

"I can't give you any of that gruel you were

going to fix because—"

"Forget the gruel!" Miss Eva yawned contentedly. "Anything will do. I'll catch another little catnap while I'm waiting." And then and there, before Molly's astonished eyes, she fell asleep.

"Well, I *never!*" Molly muttered as she closed Miss Eva's door and ran down to the kitchen. "She isn't sick," she reported to her brothers. "At least she *says* she feels fine. Still, there must be something wrong with her. Imagine Miss Eva just lying peacefully in bed, smiling! It doesn't make sense."

"I'd better call Dr. Gargle," said Malcolm, "and tell him to drop over this afternoon when we're home from school."

"Waste of time," the Toad said placidly. "He can't get her up. Nobody can."

Malcolm frowned. "Molly and I will handle this, Toad. You're too young to understand these things."

The Toad did not answer.

CHAPTER NINE

I'VE CHECKED her thoroughly," Dr. Gargle told the children that afternoon as they helped him on with his coat and escorted him to the door. "Throat's not red. No fever. Good color. Clearly she's just worn out."

"Already?" Molly looked incredulous. "She's only had us one evening!"

Dr. Gargle pursed his lips noncommittally. "She's the high-strung type, remember. These people will collapse on you before you know it! She'll be fine in a few days. The question is, how will you manage while she's laid up?"

"Goodness, Dr. Gargle, we spent all last summer on our own!" Molly reminded him.

"With no grown-ups in the house."

"I heard about that." The doctor frowned disapprovingly. "And fortunately, this is a different situation. Miss Penalty may be confined to her bed, but she's in good shape mentally and able to keep tabs on you. I'll drop in tomorrow. Meanwhile, if there's any change, call me."

No sooner had they closed the front door on Dr. Gargle than the Toad burst out, "I thought he'd *never* go! Come on! It's after four, and we've got to go down to Mr. Romaine's and get stuff for supper."

"For supper?" said Malcolm. "Why the kitchen is full of all that food Mr. Romaine delivered yesterday. We're supposed to have boiled tongue and stuffed eggplant tonight. Miss Eva has the menu for the whole week written down on the kitchen blackboard."

A hideous change passed over his little brother's features. He turned from his normal grubby pink, to brick red, and then to a blotchy purple. Noting this, Malcolm hurriedly said,

"There's no sense getting into a rage, Toad. You know it's wicked to waste good food."

"I *don't* waste good food!" snarled the Toad. "But this is *horrible* food!"

Molly sniffed in a superior way. "We don't like it a bit more than you do. But you don't hear us complaining, do you?"

"Since it's here, we must use it," said noble Malcolm.

"Okay. Let's *use* it then!" the Toad shouted in his fury. "Let's use it all you guys want! Only don't let's *eat* it!"

"Silly remarks never help!" Molly observed.

"What's silly about my remarks? You wanna know a good way to use that tongue? Okay. My cats would love it."

"That's true! They would!" Malcolm burst out. "They'd eat it and then it wouldn't be wasted!"

Molly had narrowed her eyes thoughtfully. "I don't suppose your animals would care for eggplant, too?" she inquired.

The Toad vigorously shook his head. "They hate vegetables even worse than me!"

Malcolm paced the front hall, striking his forehead with his fist. "Oh, somewhere in this world," he groaned, "there must be a good, wholesome use for eggplants and okra and stuff like rutabagas, without actually *eating* them!"

"I have it!" Molly cried. "The compost heap in the backyard! I've heard Mrs. Coverlet say a hundred times there's nothing like rotting vegetable matter to make flowers grow!"

The anxious furrows on Malcolm's brow smoothed away. "What a wonderful idea, Molly! And think how grateful Mrs. Coverlet will be next summer when her flowers are blooming better than any of the neighbors' and she can't understand why, and we tell her what we—"

"Shut up, Malcolm," interrupted the Toad. "No time to talk all day! Now that we've figured out how to get rid of all that stuff in the kitchen, let's get going to the store. We're practically out of peanut butter, you know!"

"I'll run up and tell Miss Eva we're going out," Molly said. Miss Eva lay just as she had all day, resting on pillows, wearing a blissfully drowsy expression.

"We're going down to Mr. Romaine's," Molly informed her. "We—uh—aren't too sure how you boil a tongue or stuff an eggplant, so we thought we'd get a little hamburger, just for tonight."

"How sensible! How sensible!" sighed Miss Eva. "I see I can relax and not have a moment's worry about you three. And when you're going past the drugstore, would you pick me up a paperback book? If I had a good mystery, I believe I could lie here and read and snooze, read and snooze *forever*!"

"Glad to," Molly murmured, and, noticing that Miss Eva's flickering eyelids were settling lower and lower, she softly closed the door and ran down to join her brothers.

 WEEK HAD gone by, and it was the middle of December. Amazing to tell, Miss Eva had still not stirred a step out of her room. For seven days now she had dozed and read, dozed and read, only getting up long enough to brush her hair, open or shut her window, run some water in her bathroom, or get something from a bureau drawer. Dr. Gargle admitted to the children that he was mystified by the case. Try as he would, he could find nothing wrong with Miss Eva. On the other hand, he said the rest was doing her worlds of good. Her long face was taking on a pinkish plumpness, and her eyelids, instead of constantly blinking, now opened and closed in a

placid manner which was rather agreeable to watch.

The Persever children were very satisfied with the turn of events. Miss Eva was no bother. Whenever they made a trip to Mr. Romaine's for groceries, they stopped in at Capsule's Drugstore to pick up more reading matter for her. Except for carrying up her tray, they would hardly have known she was in the house.

"Haven't things turned out beautifully!" Molly exclaimed, folding a paper napkin and laying it neatly on the supper tray she was setting for their patient. "We do just as we please. We're as free as we were this summer when we *really* were alone."

"Only this is better," Malcolm added. "We don't have to hide anything from the neighbors. Everybody's easy in their minds just knowing Miss Eva's in the house here. Mr. Forthright went off to his clergymen's meeting perfectly happy."

"I *thought* you guys would like it," declared the Toad.

Naturally Malcolm and Molly ignored this remark. If a person gave him the least encouragement, their vain little brother would have been happy to take credit for making the wind blow or the sun rise.

Molly picked up Miss Eva's tray and carried it out of the kitchen.

"Lovely, lovely, lovely!" Miss Eva murmured as Molly put it down before her on the blanket. "Hot dogs and pickles and potato chips and root beer and peppermint stick ice cream!" One of Miss Eva's strangest symptoms was that she now liked the very kind of food she had always disapproved of. "And you've brought me a new detective story! How thoughtful. Though I doubt if I'll have a chance to finish it. I really must get up tomorrow."

Molly was not alarmed at this news. Every evening Miss Eva announced she was getting up next morning, and every morning she was still in bed.

"Don't try to get up unless you feel like it," Molly said soothingly.

Miss Eva stifled a yawn. "Well, if you think you can manage by yourselves just one more day. We do seem to make out so nicely."

As Molly came downstairs she heard the front door close. Malcolm was standing in the vestibule reading a yellow piece of paper. "Cable from Dad," he muttered. "Messenger brought it. It says 'Breakdown at mine. Up to ears in repairs. Impossible to be home by December 25. Will have special super celebration in January to make up. Love, Dad.'"

The two children subsided on the bottom step of the front stairs. It was terrible news. Molly was the first to speak. There was something about the way Malcolm was clutching his hair and blowing dramatic sighs that annoyed her reasonable nature. "For Pete's sake!" she snapped, "it isn't the end of the world! There *are* children who never have *any* Christmas! All we have to do is wait a few weeks extra for ours. What's more," she said, brightening, "you can tell that Dad feels badly about this, so he'll probably buy us even more presents than we'd get on an ordinary Christmas!"

It was exactly this practical side of Molly's nature that shocked Malcolm. He gave her an outraged look. "You *would* think of that! I wasn't worried about presents. I was thinking about the Toad."

"What about him?"

"He believes in Santa Claus!"

"Lower your voice, Malcolm. He'll hear us."

"No, he won't. He's at Bobby Seemly's watching television. Don't you see, Molly? It's okay for us older ones to have Christmas in January. But the Toad thinks it *has* to come on the twenty-fifth of December. It's a magic day! How are we going to explain it to him that there's no use his hanging up his stocking Christmas Eve, when every boy and girl in Loganbury, and practically the whole world, is doing it then?"

"Break the truth to him," advised matter-of-fact Molly. "He's six and a half. *I* certainly knew by then."

"Oh, you always knew! That's the main trouble with you, Molly. Born without an imagination. I believed till I was eight!" Malcolm threw her a haughty look. Then he got to his feet, squared his jaw and declared, "No! The Toad is not going to have his happy childhood spoiled! We will have Christmas as usual in this house. Stockings! A tree! Turkey! Plum pudding! Everything! And when Dad gets back, we'll do it all over again if he likes."

"I think it's pure foolishness," was Molly's opinion. "And ever so much trouble to go through twice. But since you feel so strongly, I'll help. I'm sure we can manage. We've got all that money in the savings bank, so we can go shopping, and wrap up the things and hide them. As far as Christmas dinner is concerned, we don't need to worry about that. Mrs. Coverlet will be back by then—unless—" she looked uneasy. "Unless, she *should* win first prize in that contest and have to stay in New York for the three weeks' public appearance tour. But there isn't a chance in a thousand of *that!*"

Just then the back door slammed, and the Toad was bellowing their names as he galloped through the house. "Malcolm! Molly! She was just on TV! Oh, there you are! Why are you guys sitting on the steps in the dark?"

"*Who* was on TV?" Molly asked.

"It was the five o'clock news from New York!"

"But *who?*"

"And she was laughing and crying! They all shook her hand! The announcer was eating some!"

"Some *what?*"

"Chocolate Stale Bread Pudding! What I invented! Then they gave her a big bunch of flowers!"

"You don't mean—"

"—I do too mean! She won! She won, you dumbheads! Mrs. Coverlet!"

"*Our* Mrs. Coverlet?"

"Whose else's? What's the matter with you guys? Aren't you glad?"

"Naturally we're glad!" stammered Malcolm. "We were only thinking that she has to stay in New York now, and she won't be home for Christmas!"

The Toad's grin faded. "Poor Mrs. Coverlet!" he said. "She'll miss the best day of the year! Well, we'll just have to save her presents and tell her everything when she gets home. I'm going up to my room and tell my cats about the contest."

"Wait a sec, Toad," said Molly. "We got a cable from Dad this afternoon, and *he* won't be home for Christmas, either. Not till January."

"*Gol-lee!*" the Toad exclaimed. "The poor grown-ups!" He looked serious. "I wouldn't be away from home on Christmas Day for *anything*! Imagine having to miss Santa Claus!" He ran upstairs past Malcolm and Molly.

The two older Persevers looked apprehensively at each other. "Can we really do it all by ourselves?" Molly wondered. "Stuff a turkey? Bake pies? It seems to me Mrs. Coverlet works on Christmas for days beforehand!"

"Chin up, Molly!" her big brother encouraged her. "There are recipe books, you know. Anyway, by that time Miss Eva should surely be up, and she can take over the cooking again."

Unfortunately, this only made Molly shudder. "Oh, dear!" she said. "Christmas and Miss Eva just don't seem to go together. I'm not sure I wouldn't rather tackle Christmas all by ourselves than have Miss Eva help us."

CHAPTER ELEVEN

OU GOING TO read to me to-
night?" the Toad asked Molly
that evening as they were finishing supper.
"What would you like to hear?"

"*Twenty Thousand Leaks under the Sea.*
Want to know how they plugged up all those
holes."

"*Leagues*, Toad—not leaks. And that book
is too old for you."

"Oh it is, is it?" snarled the disrespectful
child.

Malcolm held up his hand for attention. "I
have a serious matter to discuss before we leave
this table."

"It wasn't *my* fault!" put in the Toad. "It

was the dumb milkman's."

"I'm not talking about a milkman. I want us to make up our minds whether we want a turkey or a goose for Christmas dinner." Malcolm's face was darkening suspiciously. "Hey, what *about* the milkman, Toad?"

Now that the youngest Persever saw that Malcolm knew nothing of the unfortunate incident that morning, he wished he'd kept quiet. "He tripped, is all," said the Toad, sulkily.

"On what?" his inquisitive sister had to know.

"On a little, teeny, weeny, eeny wire." The Toad held up one hand with the thumb and forefinger nearly touching, and squinted his beady brown eyes almost shut in order to peer through them. This was to show Malcolm and Molly what a small wire it was: a wire of no importance, a wire not worth bringing into any respectable conversation.

But Molly Persever went on anyway. "Teeny, weeny, eeny wire which was *where*?"

The Toad sighed. "Hanging out of my window," he grudgingly admitted. "Running over to the foot of the chestnut tree. It's my cat pulley. I invented it today. I have this basket attached to it for my cats to ride in, so I can let them in and out of the house without going downstairs."

"But if it goes from your window over to the foot of the tree," said Malcolm, appalled, "that means the wire runs right across the front walk!"

The Toad shrugged. "He ought to be looking where he's going," he grumbled. "He walked right into it and fell over backward and broke all his bottles, and then goes and blames *me*!" The Toad looked from Malcolm to Molly with an abused expression. But they only stared back at him so disapprovingly that he blurted, "Okay. Okay! I'll take it down. Let's change the subject! What were you asking about Christmas, Malcolm?"

"If we should have a goose or a turkey."

"Turkey," decided the Toad, without a second's hesitation, "because they're bigger. But, gol-lee!" he said, looking downcast and leaning his elbows on the table. "Of all years for Dad and Mrs. Coverlet to have to miss Christmas! Because," here he looked slyly at the others, "I'll tell you a secret. This Christmas we're going to have snow!"

"That is the silliest thing you've *ever* said, Theobold Persever," his sister calmly informed him. "You know we never have snow in Loganbury for Christmas!"

"We're too far south," Malcolm explained.

"Just the same, we're going to," the Toad maintained.

"Toad, it's foolish to talk like that. Even the weatherman can't tell what sort of day it will be ten days from now!"

"Well, *I* know!"

"Maybe he has a snowmaking machine hidden upstairs in his closet." Molly giggled, casting a superior smile at her younger brother. But she was disconcerted to find the Toad grinning right back at her. For a second she had a wild impulse to run right up to his room and have a look in his closet. But Molly was not the sort of person who approved of wild impulses, and the idea of a snow machine was so ridiculous she was ashamed of herself for even thinking it.

"If you're through with your dessert," she told the Toad severely, "go upstairs and untie that wire from your window before somebody breaks his neck. And tomorrow, fix your cat pulley some other way so it doesn't hang across the front walk."

As soon as he was out of the room she fumed, "What in the world gives him the idea we're having snow for Christmas?"

"It's one of his childish notions. Pay no attention. He'll forget it in a day or two."

"But he seems so *sure*! Malcolm, have you noticed anything strange about the Toad lately?"

Malcolm shook his head.

"I have the feeling he thinks he has some kind

of—well—power! That he can *make things happen*. Like the way he's always dropping hints about Miss Eva. As if he had something to do with her staying in her room out of our way."

"But that's ridiculous, Molly! How could he poss—"

"—Of course it's ridiculous! You don't think I believe it, do you? I'm only saying it's how he *feels*. And I certainly would like to know what's going on in his mind."

"Very little," Malcolm assured her. "He hasn't much mind for anything to go on in. He's only six years old, you know. It's just that being the youngest, he likes to say wild things to make himself seem important and attract attention. The best thing to do is ignore him."

Molly nodded. "I suppose you're right."

"And never argue with him when he talks that way, or show the least interest. It only encourages him." After this wise advice of Malcolm's the two older Persevers got up from the supper table and began to clear away the dishes.

CHAPTER TWELVE

HE NEXT MORNING Christmas vacation began. Directly after breakfast Malcolm and Molly left the house and walked downtown to the bank. The Persever children had all the money they had earned the summer before in a savings account. Mr. Vault, the bank manager, knew them well, and promptly handed Malcolm the thirty dollars he asked for. And now the older Persevers were ready for their Christmas shopping.

"First we go to Hammer's Hardware and get the Toad's sled," Malcolm said, putting his fat wallet back in his pocket, and leading the way across the marble bank lobby to the revolving doors.

"Sled?" protested Molly behind him. "What's the sense in *that*?" Her brother was temporarily out of earshot as he was swallowed up between the heavy doors. "What's the sense in a sled?" she repeated, coming out on the sidewalk beside him. "It isn't going to snow for Christmas, whatever the Toad says. A good express wagon would be much more practical, and we could all get some use out of it, hauling groceries home."

"He doesn't *want* a wagon. He wants a sled. It's on the top of his list."

"Don't tell me we have got to get him everything he's got on that list he wrote Santa Claus? That's going *too* far, Malcolm! Even for your conscience! Even to save the Toad's happy childhood! Where are we going to find a baby gorilla in Loganbury, may I ask? And a performing seal? And a real miniature train like they have in amusement parks to run all over our yard on little tracks?"

"Now, now, he doesn't really expect all

those things," Malcolm soothed her. "He only puts them down to test how far Santa will go."

"And by the way, Malcolm, since you and I are trying to fix Christmas so it will seem to the Toad just exactly like other Christmases when the grown-ups did it, isn't he going to think it's funny that only *his* stocking is full, and *he* has a bunch of presents and you and I don't?"

Malcolm stopped in his tracks. "What do you think I got the thirty dollars for? Ten is for us to spend on the Toad. Ten *I* keep to buy things for you. And ten you take for my presents—and keep them a secret, of course."

"Oh, I *see*!" For the first time Molly looked actually enthusiastic about Malcolm's Christmas scheme. "In that case," she reflected, as they trudged along in the direction of Hammer's Hardware, "I might mention something I saw in Nickell's Department Store the other day. It's a little chest with three drawers you can lock. I'd certainly like to have someplace I could keep my good pencils and paints and things, and not have people always borrowing them when they've lost theirs. It costs three ninety-five," she concluded helpfully.

"I'll remember," her brother remarked. "Which reminds me. Since we're stopping off at Hammer's Hardware anyway, you might notice a camping knife they've got there. It's got a separate blade for scaling fish and a magnet for pulling nails out of cracks, and a really good bottle opener. What do you know! We're here!" The two Persevers turned out of the cold December air into Mr. Hammer's warm brown store.

A few hours later they were staggering home again with various packages, including a beautiful sled which Mr. Hammer had disguised as best he could with yards of brown paper and string. And there were several mysterious parcels which Molly had bought while Malcolm looked the other way, and several more which Malcolm had bought while Molly looked the other way.

The Toad was not to be seen. But from upstairs in his room came the sound of pounding, punctuated by shouts of congratulations to himself. "That's the way to do it, Toad!" he would bellow. "One more good whack. There! That does it! Good job!"

"Fixing his cat pulley," Molly commented.

"Let's sneak upstairs and hide this stuff in my room," suggested Malcolm.

They had tiptoed safely along the upstairs hall and were just at Malcolm's door when a drowsy voice called out, "I hear you-oo-oo!"

Miss Eva had caught the rustling of all that brown paper! "Come ih-hin!" insisted the voice, pleasantly enough. The children looked at each other in dismay. Miss Eva knew about the cable from the children's father, and she knew that Mrs. Coverlet had won the baking contest. She naturally assumed that the children were waiting to celebrate Christmas in January. Malcolm and Molly were not sure she would approve of their scheme to have Christmas on their own.

"Molly and I were just doing a little shopping," Malcolm murmured, opening Miss Eva's door a crack.

"We're going to give each other a few things Christmas morning," added Molly.

"Oh, lovely! Lovely! Let me see! I adore Christmas secrets!"

Malcolm and Molly reluctantly filed into Miss Eva's room. When they came out again, a few minutes later, their arms were empty.

"I can't get over it!" said Malcolm as they were going downstairs to the kitchen to make sandwiches for lunch.

"Offering to wrap all those presents for us!"

"And keep them hidden under her bed till Christmas Eve!"

"Which is a wonderful idea!" Molly giggled. "The Toad is terrible about snooping before Christmas. But he'll never think to look *there*!"

"What did she ask you to get her pocketbook from the bureau for?"

"She gave me six dollars," Molly replied softly, opening her fingers to show Malcolm the bills. "To buy Christmas presents for the three of us. From her. Two dollars apiece. In case she isn't up and around herself in time to do it."

Malcolm sighed. "A person could almost get to like Miss Eva the way she is now. Her disposition is quite changed. It's a terrible thing to say," he added, looking guilty. "But since she's so happy in bed, and not suffering or anything, I can't help hoping that whatever's the matter with her *stays* the matter, at least till Christmas is over."

"Don't worry about that," said a confident voice from the kitchen doorway. It was the Toad, attracted from his carpentry by sounds of dishes and the slamming icebox door. "Miss Eva's in bed, and in bed she stays. Hey, who ate the last of my marshmallow sauce?"

CHAPTER THIRTEEN

*A*T TWO O'CLOCK Christmas Eve afternoon Mr. Romaine delivered the raw materials for the Persevers' Christmas dinner. Among them was a fat turkey, celery, potatoes, olives, cranberries, and for dessert, a quart of chocolate ice cream. The children had regretfully decided not to try to bake their own pies.

In the kitchen Molly was taking things out of grocery sacks and putting them away, while Malcolm had just reached down a cookbook of Mrs. Coverlet's and turned to the page headed "Roasting a Turkey."

"'Before stuffing bird,'" he read aloud, "'rub cavity with salt and butter.'"

"Cavity!" snorted his sister. "It sounds more like a dentist than a recipe!" Molly did not like to cook. And now that Christmas dinner was looming ahead, and her brothers were depending on her to know what to do because she was so practical by nature, and a girl as well, she felt quite peevish about the whole thing. She glared at the turkey, lying on its back on the counter, white and goosefleshy, legs stubbornly crossed, frozen hard as stone, and offering no help or suggestions for itself.

"There's nothing we can do with him now, anyway," Malcolm observed, prodding their bird with one finger. "He's so hard we'll have to thaw him overnight and stuff him in the morning."

Molly nodded. Out of the corner of her eye she saw the Toad tiptoeing down the back hall to the door, wearing his jacket, a hatchet in one hand and a ball of twine in the other. "May I ask where you're going?" she called out.

"Where does it look like?" Since he had

been discovered, the Toad thought he might as well bluster it out. "I'm going to find us a Christmas tree and chop it down."

"Chop down a Christmas tree! Why, Toad, you know we always get a tree from Mr. Bouncer. It's his regular Christmas present to the employees of the vitamin company. The truck ought to be stopping around with it any minute."

"Oh yeah?" the Toad replied. "Dad's on a leave of absence now. He isn't working for Mr. Bouncer so we don't get any tree this year."

Molly and Malcolm exchanged a disconcerted glance. Neither of them had thought of that. Mr. Bouncer's tree, delivered all rustling, all fragrant, and sticky with resin, by a couple of jolly men, had been a part of Christmas Eve ever since they could remember.

"We'd better get our jackets on and go right down to that tree lot behind Capsule's Drugstore," Malcolm said soberly, "while there are some trees left."

The Toad beetled his brow. "Why *can't* I chop one down?"

"Because," explained Malcolm, "there aren't any woods around Loganbury, and the evergreens growing in people's yards belong to them."

"What if I got a tree that doesn't belong to anybody?"

"Where, for heaven's sake?" demanded Molly.

"At the slough." This was a thickety, marshy area not more than a mile from the Persevers'. In warm weather the Persevers often went there to have picnics and catch turtles and explore. As far as they knew, nobody owned the place. Nobody but themselves ever used it, except for people who occasionally would back their cars as far as they dared down the muddy lane which led to it and dump garden trash or empty paint cans into the water.

"Do you mean to say you know of a pine tree down at the slough?" Molly asked incredulously.

"Not exactly *know* of one," the Toad admitted, "but I'm sure there must be one, and if there is, I can find it."

"There is nothing growing at the slough but willows and alders and horrible prickers and briars wherever you step," Molly insisted. "It's a stupid waste of time to go there."

Malcolm pointed out to her under his breath that there was nothing they could do just then about Christmas dinner, and, the presents being all wrapped and hidden under Miss Eva's bed, they might just as well get out in the fresh air and go with the Toad to the slough. "After all," he whispered, "it's Christmas Eve, and we're trying to give him a happy time to remember. We can always stop off at that tree lot on our way home."

"All right, all right," Molly sighed, giving in against her better judgment.

A few minutes later the Persevers were on their way. Malcolm had insisted on carrying the hatchet and this annoyed the Toad. He brought up the rear of the procession muttering under his breath. "Might've known! Let those guys in on any of my good ideas and they have to run the show!"

As they marched along, up one side of Loganbury Hill and down the other to where the houses grew more scattered, the Toad's spirits bubbled up again. "Good thing we started when we did," he told the others, "before the snow begins." It was a blue and gold afternoon, with not so much as a fleck of a cloud in the sky, and the winter sun was winking and glittering on every roof and window. The Toad's remark about snow was so preposterous that Molly and Malcolm did not bother to reply.

When they came to the place in the road where you turn down a rutted lane to the slough, the Toad dashed ahead. "I got to fix something," he shouted back.

Molly and Malcolm, following more sedately, could see their little brother ahead, picking his way along the muddy bank of the slough. When he reached a certain willow tree bending over the water, he cut off a long straight twig with his pocketknife. Then, holding the slender stick straight before him, he closed his eyes, slowly turned in a circle three times, his lips moving all the while.

"What kind of silliness do you call that?" Molly inquired as they came up to him.

The Toad did not answer until he had finished the third circle. Then he opened his eyes wide and called in great excitement, "This way, you guys!" With his willow stick pointing straight before him, the Toad started toward a dense thicket and was swallowed from view in alders and vines. Molly and Malcolm came along behind him, stumbling over rotting logs, into holes, through briars, under branches, and around stumps.

"This is what comes of humoring him!" Molly fumed as she heard a ripping noise in the sleeve of her red corduroy jacket. They could not see their little brother through the tangle, but they could plainly hear him crashing about.

Then he gave a shout, and all grew silent ahead.

"What's happened? Are you okay?" Malcolm called in alarm. He and Molly plunged into a particularly bristling barrier of briars and emerged into a sunny clearing carpeted with yellow grass. There sat the Toad modestly twirling his willow stick, and beside him stood a Christmas tree, the most feather-leafed, glossy, cone-shaped, pointy-topped tree they had ever seen.

"Well?" said the Toad, as his brother and sister panted and stared. "You've got the hatchet, Malcolm. Are you going to chop it down or not?"

"What *I* don't understand," Molly burst out, looking keenly at the Toad, "is why you didn't tell us about this tree. You knew it was here all the time! You came straight to it!"

The Toad smiled mysteriously. "I never saw

it before. I never was *here* before. It was my willow wand that found it."

"What kind of a remark is that?" demanded Molly in exasperation.

"Stop arguing, you two!" Malcolm insisted. "I need you both to stand over on the other side to catch her as she falls."

The oldest Persever stepped forward, knelt down beside the tree, and the sound of the hatchet rang out. When the tree began to lean, Molly and the Toad eased it down. Then they wrapped the branches round and round with twine to make it more convenient to carry.

"Pick up your end, Toad!" Malcolm ordered as he and Molly hoisted the heavy end, the one with the trunk.

The Toad lifted the nodding, pointed tip of the tree, and they started toward the place in the surrounding thicket which seemed least overgrown.

"Boy, oh boy, oh *boy*!" exclaimed the Toad, strutting along in the lead. "This is the way to get a Christmas tree! The cheapest! The smartest! The best!"

"I wouldn't be too sure of that!" rumbled a deep, strange voice, invisible in the thicket. The three Persevers stopped in their tracks and looked about them. A branch snapped, and out into their pretty little clearing stepped a fat man in shabby clothes and a slouch hat. "Stand right where you are, my young friends," he said grimly. "Where did you think you were going with my spruce?"

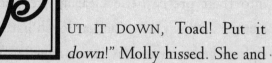

CHAPTER FOURTEEN

"PUT IT DOWN, Toad! Put it *down*!" Molly hissed. She and Malcolm had dropped their end of the tree the instant the man appeared. But their little brother, eyes round as two yo-yos, was clutching his with both arms against his chest. "What is the meaning of this?" demanded the fat man, coming close. He seized the tree from the Toad's grasp, stood it up, looked at it bitterly, and shook his head. "One of my finest young spruces! There aren't more than three on the whole property!"

The more Malcolm looked at the stranger, the more he was certain that he had seen him before, but for the life of him he could not place him in that funny slouch hat. "Oh, sir!" gulped the Persever with a conscience. "We had no idea the slough belonged to anyone!"

"It belongs to someone, all right! I bought it from the town this fall. It's been a disgrace to Loganbury for years. I'm doing some draining and clearing here. Then I'll turn it back to the town for a park. When I have a few hours I like to come out here and tramp around. And let me tell you, I saw red when I heard an ax from over this way!" He glowered at Malcolm's hatchet. "Do your parents have any idea what you're up to this afternoon?"

"No, sir!" Malcolm replied emphatically.

"Then I think we'll take the evidence along and go to your house and tell them!"

"But, sir," Molly put in, "our parents—you see—we have no mother, and our father is away."

"Thousands of miles away!" the Toad piped up, hoping to discourage the man.

The man looked sharply at the three children in their torn and muddy clothes. "No parents? Who looks after you?"

"We have a neighbor staying in our house," explained Molly.

"But she doesn't know a thing about our cutting down this tree," Malcolm hurriedly added. It was the only decent thing to say.

"Miss Eva doesn't know anything about *anything* we do!" the Toad proudly informed the stranger. He felt bolder now, having noticed that the more they talked, the more curious the man seemed about them and the less angry.

"And why doesn't she?" asked the man.

"Because she has to stay up in her bed all the time," the Toad said smugly.

"In bed! My word!" The man laid the tree carefully on the ground and sat down beside it on the yellow grass. "And it's Christmastime!" they heard him murmur. "Tell me," he asked, "is she very ill?"

"We don't know what's the matter with her," Molly explained. "The doctor can't figure it out. She isn't uncomfortable or anything. She just seems to be slightly bedridden."

The stranger's eyebrows rose out of sight behind his hat, and then he looked away. "So you came out here to find a Christmas tree by yourselves." He seemed uncomfortable. "Do the authorities know about your case?"

"Authorities?" Malcolm was bewildered.

"Welfare people," the man said. "The people who give Christmas baskets and clothing to the needy." In great embarrassment he was trying not to seem to notice the great tear in Molly's jacket or the patches in the Toad's pants. How could he know that Mrs. Coverlet had tried to throw away those old trousers a half-dozen times and that the Toad always rooted them out of the ragbag because he loved them so!

The children looked at each other. It was clear that the man supposed them to be charity cases. Malcolm drew himself up haughtily. "We didn't *have* to chop down the tree," he said. "We could have bought one in the usual way. We only thought this would be more adventurous. We are sorry we did it, and we will pay you for it."

Practical Molly felt a little irritated at her brother's proud words. After all, if the man wanted to jump to the wrong conclusion and pity them, it wasn't their fault! If Malcolm didn't spoil everything, the man was probably going to let them keep the tree, and since it had already been chopped down, it might as well be used.

But the Toad hated being felt sorry for even more than Malcolm did. He stuck out his small chest, put his chin in the air, and declared, "Us guys aren't poor! We've got more than a thousand dollars in the bank that we earned last summer! And who needs Christmas baskets? Santa is coming tonight!"

For some reason the Toad's words had exactly the wrong effect on the stranger. He looked more distressed than ever. It was obvious he believed the Toad was inventing the thousand dollars, and that he thought the children terribly brave and terribly proud.

"Listen!" insisted the Toad at his wits' end. "Our father owns the biggest tin mine in the world!" This was not true. Mr. Persever's tin mine was the *smallest* in the world.

It humiliated Molly to hear a brother of hers making a fool of himself, and she gave him an invisible pinch.

Still the Toad was not to be stopped. "Quit pinching me, Molly! Our Dad is also the best vitamin salesman in the world. His boss, Mr. Bouncer, says so! And Mr. Bouncer is the richest man in this town!"

"Bouncer!" The stranger gave a start. "Tin mine! Vitamin salesman! Good Lord! You children must be the Persevers!" To their astonishment, the man sitting on the grass began to laugh violently. His eyes watered. He rocked back and forth, slapping his knees. "I should have known—who else?" They watched him anxiously until the fit had passed and he was able to bring out a handkerchief and wipe his perspiring forehead.

Malcolm stared. The minute the stranger took off his slouch hat and he saw that shiny bald head, he knew who it was. "Mr. Bouncer! Oh, Mr. Bouncer, it's *you*! My dad pointed you out to me at the factory once. But you looked so different in your regular clothes."

"And you are Malcolm, of course. And this is Molly. And here is the Toad himself. I ought to have known. I've heard enough about you from your father!" Mr. Bouncer collapsed in a fresh attack of laughter. This time his recovery came sooner, and he got to his feet, lifting the trunk of the spruce tree as he did so, and saying to Malcolm, "Grab the other end, my boy! We'll take it to my car and I'll give you a lift home."

"You mean we get to keep the tree?" blundered the tactless Toad.

"Why not?" replied Mr. Bouncer. "It's already chopped down. Besides, I give the Persever family a Christmas tree every year, don't I?" Here he looked a little puzzled and hurt. "That's the one thing about all this I don't understand. I've been sending you a tree every Christmas since you were all born. Why did you think you had to get your own this year?"

"Well, with Dad on leave of absence—" began Malcolm.

"—We thought we'd be crossed off your list," concluded the Toad bluntly.

"And risk offending the best vitamin salesman in the world by forgetting his family?" Mr. Bouncer shook his head vehemently. "But you weren't taking any chances, were you! Came and found your own tree, and then it was Mr. Bouncer's after all." Chuckling to himself at this joke, their father's boss led the way into the thicket at the same place he had come out of it. To the children's surprise there was a path there which led to the rutted lane by the water. They were cold and tired after their adventurous afternoon, and the sight of Mr. Bouncer's red station wagon parked at the end of the lane was the most welcome thing they had seen in a long time.

CHAPTER FIFTEEN

I GOT TO ride back here with the tree and guard it!" announced the Toad, jumping up on the tailgate and putting one arm protectively over the spruce tree which hung out a few feet over the back.

Malcolm and Molly got into the front seat next to Mr. Bouncer. They too would have preferred to ride in back with their legs dangling over the tailgate. But, considering what a good sport Mr. Bouncer had been about the whole tree business, it seemed more polite to keep him company. As the car rolled along they could hear the raucous strains of the Toad's voice singing Christmas carols to himself in his own peculiar way. First it was his next to favorite, "Dig the Holes with Trowels by Golly!" And then it was his very favorite, "Good King Wences' Car Backed Out, on a Piece of Stephen."

"What *is* your brother singing?" asked Mr. Bouncer, looking into his rearview mirror in perplexity.

"Pay no attention," Malcolm advised. "He can't get anything straight."

"He's six and a half," Molly confessed, "but he's not very bright for his age."

"Hm-m-m," said Mr. Bouncer. Presently their father's boss remarked that he had always understood that the Persevers had a wonderful housekeeper who looked after them, and how did it happen that a neighbor was staying with them? Malcolm and Molly explained about the White Blizzard Flour Contest.

"Extraordinary!" said Mr. Bouncer, when he had heard. "But about tomorrow. Suppose this neighbor of yours, Miss Penalty, still isn't on her feet. How on earth will you ever manage Christmas by yourselves?"

"Don't worry about us," Molly assured him. "We've thought of everything."

"It was our own idea to fix Christmas tomorrow," Malcolm explained. "Dad promised us a celebration when he gets back. But the thing of it was," he lowered his voice confidentially, "the Toad *believes*! We couldn't let tomorrow come without doing something."

"My word, of course you couldn't!" Mr. Bouncer saw that at once. "But have you bought presents and all?"

"Yes," Malcolm said. "We got the Toad a sled for one thing. It's crazy, but he keeps telling us he knows there'll be snow for Christmas."

As the three of them in the front seat looked through the windshield at the sun going down in a cloudless, orange sky, they chuckled at the thought of snow falling that night. Mr. Bouncer still seemed unconvinced about the children's Christmas plans as he drew up in front of their house. "About Christmas dinner," he asked, turning off the motor, "do you mean you've bought all the fixings and are cooking it your-selves?"

The Toad jumped off the tailgate, came around the car, and stuck his head through the window next to Malcolm.

"We've thought of everything," Molly was saying to Mr. Bouncer, "turkey, cranberries, potatoes—"

"—But not a plum pudding!" interrupted the Toad, looking accusingly in at his sister.

"What?" Mr. Bouncer looked appalled. "No plum pudding for Christmas?"

"See! I told you we should have one!" said the Toad.

"And I told you that Dad is the only one in the family who knows about making it flame, and we aren't going to risk burning the house down!"

Mr. Bouncer got out of the car, went around to the back, and pulled out the Christmas tree.

"Tsk, tsk, no pudding," he repeated sadly to himself as he and Malcolm carried it up the steps and along the walk to the porch. "No plum pudding for Christmas! What a pity!" He leaned the tree against the house thoughtfully, then snapped his fingers as an idea came to him. "Listen! Why don't I stop around here tomorrow with a pudding and a little brandy to light her up?"

"Br-*andy*!" Malcolm looked horribly shocked. "Mr. Bouncer! Remember, we're *children*!"

"My dear boy, in the case of Christmas pudding, brandy is perfectly respectable. It's all burned up in the blue flame, you see!"

"Are you positive? I'm responsible for the younger ones, you know."

"Guarantee it. Brandy's what your father uses, after all."

"Oh, well, in *that* case!" Malcolm looked relieved.

"We'd love it if you'd come tomorrow!"

Molly urged Mr. Bouncer. "Then you'd get to see your spruce tree all decorated, too!"

"We shouldn't take Mr. Bouncer away from his family on Christmas Day," Malcolm reproved his sister.

"To tell the truth, you wouldn't be!" Mr. Bouncer confessed. "Mrs. Bouncer is in Memphis visiting our married son. I was to fly there and join them, but at the last minute I couldn't get away from the vitamin plant. So I'll just be going down to the Loganbury Hotel for Christmas dinner, I suppose."

"Oh, Mr. Bouncer, why don't you have Christmas dinner with us?" Molly exclaimed impetuously.

Mr. Bouncer tried to hide his pleasure. "Now, my dear, I couldn't dream of intruding."

"Yes, please come!" Malcolm said. "Mr. Forthright will be here, I think. He isn't back from his trip yet, but he always has Christmas dinner with us."

"Well, if you insist," beamed Mr. Bouncer.

And so it was settled, and Mr. Bouncer drove away in his red station wagon, while the three children waved to him from the porch.

The Toad sighed. "I just hope there'll be enough turkey," he muttered darkly as they turned to go inside.

His sister gave him an outraged look. "What a selfish child!"

"After we cut down his good tree and he helped us home with it and is bringing a plum pudding tomorrow!" Malcolm added.

The Toad shrugged. "I didn't say he wasn't a nice man. I just said I hoped there'd be enough turkey. Goodness knows, Mr. Forthright eats enough, but Mr. Bouncer is *huge*. I bet he eats like an elephant."

"Then the rest of us can have smaller pieces," Molly snapped. "I never saw a stupider boy!"

"Stupid!" the Toad bellowed. "If it hadn't been for me you wouldn't have this beautiful tree at all! And if I hadn't mentioned the plum pudding to Mr. Bouncer, we wouldn't be getting that, either! It's a good thing I'm here. You two wouldn't be able to get ready for Christmas at *all* if it weren't for me. Stupid boy! Hah!" He flung open the front door, stalked inside, and went clumping upstairs to his room to see his cats.

It was too much for Molly! When she thought of the trouble they had been to to make Christmas for this boastful little brother, the secret trips downtown to buy things, that hot, messy cooking which lay ahead tomorrow, and their adventure this afternoon which might have turned out very differently had Mr. Bouncer *not* been Mr. Bouncer, it made her so exasperated that she pushed by Malcolm and started into the house to give the Toad a piece of her mind.

Malcolm put his hand on her shoulder. "Never mind what he says," he soothed her. "He's only six. Don't spoil everything now. It's Christmas Eve. Look!" He pointed over the porch railing. It was almost dark. Christmas lights were coming on at almost every house along the street and up the hill away from them; from gaudy wreaths of colored bulbs on door-ways and eaves to shimmering glimpses of candles behind curtains.

"Help me with this tree," came Malcolm's voice behind her. So Molly turned and lifted the rustling tree, and they carried it indoors together.

CHAPTER SIXTEEN

I 'VE FINISHED THE tree stand," Malcolm called from the living room to Molly and the Toad, who were doing the supper dishes in the kitchen. "Come on in if you want to see the tree go up!" He began to raise the spruce from the floor.

"Oh! Stop!" Molly yelled, coming through the doorway. "It's too tall!" The top branches were brushing the ceiling, and the tree was not nearly erect. What a discovery! The spruce tree had not seemed very big as it stood in the clearing behind the slough. But it was two or three feet too high for the Persevers' living room. Malcolm laid it back on the floor and frowned.

The Toad ran across the room and took a

fierce stand between his brother and the pros-
trate Christmas tree. "I know what you're
thinking," he snarled. "And don't do it! My
tree's been through enough for one day. If I'd
thought you guys would try to shorten it, I
never would have found it for you. Poor tree!"

"Don't be ridiculous!" snapped Molly. "If
the top has to be trimmed, it has to be trimmed."

"It doesn't either! We can just as well cut a
nice round hole in the living room ceiling."

"Hole in the *ceiling*!" Malcolm groaned at
such a suggestion. "Do you want to ruin the
house? Anyway, whose bedroom do you think is
on top of us? Miss Eva's!"

"So what if it is? All the better! Since Miss
Eva can't come down and see the Christmas
tree, it would be very thoughtful of us to stick
it up through the floor so she can enjoy one end
of it!"

"Out of the way, Toad!" Malcolm ordered,
ignoring him, and getting down on his knees
beside the tree with his saw. "Steady her,

Molly." The Toad closed his beady little eyes, clapped his hands over his ears, and began to roar. However, the operation went ahead, and a moment later Malcolm exclaimed, "There we are!"

The Toad opened one eye. There lay the beheaded tree, and Malcolm was proudly holding up what had been the top of it which now looked like a second, miniature Christmas tree, two and a half feet tall.

Molly looked critically at the sawed-off end of the big spruce. "It's a little flat and bushy right now," she observed, "but I can fix that." The sensible girl trotted off to the basement and returned a minute later with a pair of garden shears. She snipped the top branches all around to narrow and shape them; and when Malcolm once again raised the spruce on its stand, it missed the ceiling neatly and looked so beautiful and natural that nobody would have guessed it hadn't grown that way.

"I'll make a base for the little tree," said

Malcolm, "and we'll decorate it for Miss Eva's bedside table."

The Toad, who only a moment before had been howling in indignation, was strutting about the living room, his hands behind his back, beaming first at the big tree, and then at the small one.

"What are you looking so pleased with yourself for?" Molly asked him.

"Because that was such a good idea of mine to cut off the top," he told his sister modestly. "It took brains to think of that! But I knew it would work."

Malcolm and Molly gave him hard looks, but of course he paid no attention. By now he was on the floor opening the boxes of Christmas ornaments, and throwing tissue paper over his shoulder. "Here are the walnuts we painted gold! Here's the angel for the top! Here are the silver bells that don't really ring! Heck, there's one broken! Come help me, you guys!"

But to tell the truth, the first sight of these

dear old ornaments, which the older Persevers remembered from the days when the Toad had been a baby, pierced them with lonesomeness and doubt. Recalling all the other Christmases of their lives, with their father and Mrs. Coverlet taking charge of everything, Molly and Malcolm wondered if it hadn't been a rash mistake to try to celebrate it on their own. But a person couldn't stay sad for long in the same room with the joyful Toad.

"Here's the ornament I swallowed!" he called out triumphantly, holding up a green glass acorn, tarnished and chipped with age. "Mrs. Coverlet turned me upside down and pounded me till it popped up! I know it's the one because Dad tied a thread on the hook so I could always tell!" The Toad jumped up and hung his green acorn in a prominent place on the tree.

When both trees were decorated, the children formed a procession to take the little one upstairs to Miss Eva. Malcolm was in the lead, holding the tree loaded with lights and balls, and tinkling with every step he took. Nobody answered when they knocked on the spare room door, so Molly opened it, and they saw that Miss Eva was asleep. Her supper tray was pushed to the end of the bed, and her detective book was lying across the blanket. They tiptoed inside, and Malcolm set the tinkling tree on the table next to her bed.

"Plug in the lights!" Molly whispered, and then she sighed, "How beautiful!" when the blue and silver and green glow fell on the wall and Miss Eva's pillow.

"She looks so peaceful—and—harmless!" Malcolm murmured, looking down at Miss Eva, asleep.

"Like a princess under a spell," breathed Molly.

At her words, the Toad let out a snort. Horrified, Malcolm put his hand over his brother's mouth and they hurried him out.

"What's so funny?" they asked when they had him safely in the hall.

"Spell's okay! But—hee hee—some princess!"

"I think you're disgusting!" his sister told him frankly. "Now let's hang up the stockings, because it's time for you to go to bed."

The Persevers always used their father's enormous gray hunting stockings at Christmas, since they were the roomiest in the house. When they had tacked three of them against the mantelpiece, Malcolm turned off all the living room lights except the ones on the tree, and the children sat in a row on the hearth looking around their familiar room which had taken on its special misty and magical Christmas quality.

The lights made overlapping pools of rose and emerald and silver on the ceiling, and shadows of huge, shaggy black branches on the walls, as if the children's spruce were not the only tree and they were really sitting in an enchanted forest.

The Toad hugged his knees in bliss. And then he sighed. "What a shame the grown-ups had to miss Christmas!"

"Not miss, exactly. Just have it late," Malcolm said.

"Late isn't the same. Oh, I wouldn't miss the real one for *anything*!"

"Time for bed, Toady," his sister reminded him gently.

To their surprise he jumped up without arguing. But it was Christmas Eve, and he had good reasons for wanting to get the night over with. As he passed the front window he pressed his nose against the glass and they heard him exclaim, "A snowflake! I told you! I told you!"

Malcolm and Molly ran to the window. There was nothing to be seen but a black night, Christmas lights, and patches of brown ground, lit up by the street lamps.

"I sure hope Santa hasn't forgotten my sled," remarked the dauntless Toad.

"Go to bed, Toady," Malcolm said patiently. "And don't count too much on snow!"

"Oh, I'm not worried!" came his cheerful voice from the stairs.

CHAPTER SEVENTEEN

**A**FTER THEY HAD waited down-
stairs until everything was
quiet in the Toad's room, and then another ten
minutes to make sure he was really asleep,
Malcolm and Molly tiptoed up to Miss Eva's
room and drew all the presents from under the
bed without waking her. They arranged them
under their beautiful spruce tree to look like as
many packages as possible.

Next they opened the three shopping bags
they had filled the afternoon before at the five-
and-ten, and got to work filling the stockings.
One of the shopping bags had things just for the
Toad, so they stuffed his stocking together.
Then they turned their backs on each other

while Malcolm filled Molly's stocking with the surprises he had bought for her—including a set of jacks, a bottle of bubble bath, a green leather pocket notebook, and a pack of cards; and Molly filled Malcolm's with such items as a retractable pencil with both red and black lead, a jar of plastic glue, a new toothbrush (which she happened to know he needed), and a paper stapler (which she'd always felt would be useful in the house and hoped to be able to borrow from him).

When they were through, they looked around their festive living room one last satisfied time, and Molly yawned, and Malcolm got down on his knees to turn off the Christmas tree lights. All at once there was a knock at the front door.

"What on earth?" Molly gasped. "It's after ten o'clock!"

It was the Reverend Forthright, home from his clergymen's meeting in time for Christmas. "Hi, kids!" he exclaimed, stepping inside with an armful of presents. "Got back this afternoon, but there wasn't a minute to run over here before. Had to go straight over to the church and check with my assistant to see how things had gone, and then we had the Christmas Eve Candlelight Service till just now." He laid his packages under the Christmas tree along with the others. "What a tree!" he said admiringly, as he straightened up. "Most beautiful one you've ever had, I'd say." He was peering about the Persevers' living room in an expectant way. "Where's your father? I thought you children would be in bed by now."

"He's still in New Zealand, Mr. Forthright. He isn't here."

"Still at the tin mine? At Christmastime? I don't believe it!"

"There was an emergency again. He'll be back in January, and we'll celebrate Christmas all over."

"From the looks of this room I see that you and Mrs. Coverlet are going right ahead with a regular Christmas anyway."

"Not exactly," Malcolm admitted. "Mrs. Coverlet isn't here either. You see, she *won* the White Blizzard Flour Contest and she's still in New York on a publicity tour."

Mr. Forthright collapsed in a chair. "Then Miss Eva has been holding the fort here with you all this time? A little longer visit than anybody counted on." He lowered his voice. "How have you all been getting along?"

"Oh, fine, Mr. Forthright! It's been perfect!" Molly told him. "Miss Eva's been in bed since the first morning she moved in."

"Sick all this time?"

"—Not exactly sick," Malcolm reassured him. "She just seems to *feel* like staying in bed."

"Dr. Gargle can't find anything wrong," Molly added. "He comes every few days to try again. He thinks it's just the strain of looking after us."

"Her appetite is wonderful."

"She's no trouble."

"You could go up and see her, only she's asleep."

"But the tree—" Mr. Forthright murmured, looking about, "and the presents, and the stockings—"

"We did it ourselves."

The Reverend Forthright looked at the glimmering room filled with the green smell of the tree and said nothing.

"We wouldn't have gone to all this fuss just for the two of us," Malcolm said, a little embarrassed. "Molly and I would have waited for Dad and Mrs. Coverlet. But the Toad would never have understood."

"Understood what?" asked Mr. Forthright.

"Why it wasn't Christmas on Christmas Day," Molly explained.

"He's only six," Malcolm said apologetically, "and he still *believes*."

"Malcolm was afraid it might warp his whole childhood," added Molly earnestly.

"I see, I see."

"I'm worried about one thing though," Malcolm confessed. "The Toad is positive it's going to snow for tomorrow. He's going to be wild if it doesn't."

Mr. Forthright sighed. "Well, I really don't see how you two can produce snow for him. You're not magicians, no matter how well meaning you are." He smiled fondly at them and got to his feet. "It's late. We ought to be in bed. Listen, I've got a wonderful idea for tomorrow. As soon as church is over, I'll come around and see Miss Eva. Then I'll take you children down to the Loganbury Hotel for Christmas dinner. Miss Eva, too, if she's up. I'd invite everybody down to my house, only I haven't been home long enough to have much food on hand."

"But, Mr. *Forthright*!" Molly looked a little insulted. "We're expecting you here for Christmas dinner. You *always* come to our house."

"Surely you children aren't planning to cook a Christmas dinner by yourselves?"

"The turkey is unfreezing in the kitchen right this minute," Malcolm informed him proudly. "Mr. Bouncer's coming, too. His family's away."

"I'm too astonished to protest," said Mr. Forthright. "I'll be delighted to join you. Not empty-handed, either. Mrs. Seemly baked me a little ham this afternoon for a combination Welcome Home and Christmas present. Not a feast in itself, but it will be tasty with the turkey." He put on his overcoat and started toward the door. "Till tomorrow, old friends," he said, an arm around both the children's shoulders.

When they had said good-night, Mr. Forthright stood alone on the Persevers' porch buttoning his coat. Then he turned, looked back at the front door with its green bough which Malcolm had nailed there, and the red ribbon Molly had tied to it, and said, "God bless this house, and the children keeping Christmas in it!"

He had run down the steps and started along the walk toward the street when something soft as a moth, and cold, brushed his cheek and stuck there. Dozens more hit his face when he turned it up. "Bless my soul!" Mr. Forthright laughed out loud as he saw that the street lamps and all the Christmas lights were growing more and more blurred as if he were looking at them through a white, whirling fog. "The Toad was right! It's snowing like anything!"

CHAPTER EIGHTEEN

THERE NEVER HAD been such a snowstorm in the history of Loganbury as the one which fell that Christmas Eve. Fireplugs were drowned in it, and bushes and stumps, and all the wagons and toys children had forgotten to bring in when night came.

On Christmas morning, when it was scarcely light, a small pajama-clad figure was already racing back and forth between Malcolm's and Molly's bedrooms. It pulled at their blankets and bellowed into their ears, "Get up! Get up! Didn't believe me, huh? Look outside and see!" The oldest Persever opened one protesting eye, but when he glimpsed the white blanket weighing down the Billiards' roof, just outside his window, he leaped out of bed and ran over to see.

"It must be three feet deep!" he gasped. "Looks like it's stopped now."

"Din I tell you? Din I tell you!" blustered the Toad. "Din I tell you it would snow for Christmas? I gotta go down and see if Santa remembered my sled!" Away he rushed.

Malcolm, buttoning his shirt, met Molly coming out of her room. "Did you ever see such snow?" she whispered. "How could he have known?"

There was no time to answer before the Toad was pounding up the stairs. "I got it awright," he told them triumphantly. "Come see! Exactly the kind I wanted. Bet you guys never saw such a sled!"

"I'm going to stuff the turkey and get it into the oven," Molly announced after she had admired the sled, as if she'd never laid eyes on it. "It must be thawed by now." But she had no sooner disappeared into the kitchen than her brothers heard her shriek. And as they hurried after her, something small, black, and fat—it was John Napkin, the bad kitten—squeezed past the boys' ankles in the kitchen doorway and ran for the stairs.

"Look! Just look!" Molly was gasping. "Our beautiful turkey!"

Malcolm approached the kitchen counter and stared. "Why, it's all *shaggy*! What could have happened to it?"

"I'll tell you what's happened to it!" Molly sputtered. "The Toad's cats have been chewing on it all night!"

"How do you know it was my cats?" demanded the Toad. "It looks like moths to me. Last spring my old sweater looked just like—"

"—*Moths!*" Molly gave him a scorching glance. "John Napkin was still gnawing on it when I walked in!"

"Well, it's not my cats' fault! You guys shouldn't have left a turkey sitting out all night!"

"It was *thawing*!" Molly exploded. "And *you* know you're supposed to keep your bedroom door closed at night with those cats in with you. They always get into mischief when you don't!" She turned away from her little brother and looked disconsolately at the bird. "Oh, Malcolm, what can we *do*? The legs are picked to the bone! It wasn't a very big turkey to start with! And with Mr. Forthright and Mr. Bouncer coming—"

"Heck, there's lots of meat left," the Toad insisted, peering closely at the tattered turkey. "It's just the legs, and some of the—"

"*Just* the legs!" Malcolm protested. "They're the part I like best."

"And it looks so ugly," Molly groaned. "How can I put it on the table like that?"

"Oh, if it's the *looks* you mind, I can fix *that*!" The Toad skipped out of the kitchen and was shortly back with two big, gold acorns from the Christmas tree. He pulled off the hooks and fitted the hollow ornaments over both bare leg bones. "See!" he reassured them in a pleased voice. "Little boots! Very pretty. I'll get you a round ball for the neck if you like!"

"Oh *stop* it, Toad!" his sister exclaimed, plucking off the gold ornaments in exasperation. "Silliness won't help! Our turkey's ruined. Ruined! Ruined!"

Fortunately, Malcolm did not take such a gloomy view of things. "Listen," he said, "let's stuff it and slather it with plenty of butter and roast it anyway. Maybe it won't look so queer when it's cooked. There's quite a bit of meat still on it, and with Mr. Forthright's ham we'll make out."

"There's nothing else we *can* do," Molly sighed as she picked up the poor, shaggy turkey and carried it to the sink.

"Hey, what are you *doing*?" The Toad opened his little brown eyes wide in horror. "Not *washing* it, Molly? Help! Not soap, too?" The Toad had little use for water and none at all for soap. "You don't have to do that! My cats' mouths are clean. They lick me all the time and I'm *fine!*"

"It's *because* they lick you that I have to wash the *turkey!*" snapped Molly disagreeably.

Even Malcolm was a little taken aback at the thoroughness of Molly's work. "I don't think you need to scrub it all that hard," he suggested. "You'll take all the flavor out. By the time it bakes three or four hours the germs should be dead."

At last, in spite of her two brothers, Molly had washed and dried the turkey to her satisfaction, stuffed it and buttered it all over, laid it in a roasting pan, and shut it out of sight in the oven. "Thank goodness *that's* done!" she sighed. "Let's have breakfast."

Everybody's dispositions were improved by cornflakes and sliced bananas. And presently they were back in the living room opening their presents. All the things from Mr. Forthright came from Boston where he had been for his clergymen's meeting. There was a Chinese puzzle for Malcolm, a pillow stuffed with aromatic balsam for Molly, and a plush mouse for the Toad which wound up with a key and scuttled about in a lifelike way on the rug and was greatly appreciated by Heather and the kittens.

Next, there were the stockings to empty. And after that, Molly unwrapped the box with locking drawers which she had mentioned to Malcolm, and Malcolm opened the camper's knife from Hammer's Hardware which he had pointed out to Molly. Lying under the tree, to both the older Persevers' surprise, were two unfamiliar, crudely wrapped presents for them, which came from the Toad himself. They were just alike: two packages of chocolate cigarettes, which by a strange coincidence were the Toad's favorite candy. No sooner had Malcolm and Molly opened them than their little brother helped himself freely from both packages, "just to see if the chocolate's okay."

At last there was nothing more to open. The fireplace was stuffed with wrappings. The Toad jumped to his feet, announced that the time had come to try out his sled, and departed for his room to dress. When he came back, in leggings and boots and earmuffs, he leaned against the living room door, surveyed his brother and sister with a triumphant expression, and slowly drew on his mittens.

"I'm going to tell you guys a secret," he said at last. It was Christmas, and everything had turned out so splendidly that the Toad was feeling quite kindly toward Malcolm and Molly. Besides that, he was too pleased with himself to keep his wonderful secret another moment. "You see," he confided, "it was me who made it snow." He glanced expectantly at their faces for signs of amazement.

Unfortunately, all Molly did was purse her lips and turn away. As for Malcolm, he surveyed the Toad with a look of moral disapproval and said, "You are getting too old to invent stories."

The Toad turned red on the edges of his

ears. "I did make it snow! With my magic kit!"

"Magic kit!" sniffed Molly.

The Toad's eyebrows beetled ominously. "Yeah. Magic kit. I sent in for it from the back of a horror comic."

"Aha!" Molly burst out with a meaningful look at Malcolm. "Didn't I tell you he'd cut something off the back cover of that awful thing?"

Malcolm refused to be upset on Christmas morning. "What in the world do you get when you send away for a magic kit?" he asked in an indulgent, big brotherly voice.

"Well, they sent me a booklet for one thing, with spells and charms written in it, and directions."

"Directions for what?" asked Molly, one side of her mouth pulled up in a condescending smile.

"For making a willow wand, for instance. How to choose it and cut it, and the right words to say to it so it will find what you want—like buried treasure, or anything you've lost, or just something you'd like to have. That's how I found our Christmas tree at the slough!" The Toad beamed proudly at them, but Malcolm and Molly were unimpressed.

"And there are directions for making different kinds of weather," the Toad went on, "hurricanes and blizzards and everything! Whew! Changing weather is hard work! I had to say my spells every night for *weeks* to make sure it would snow. Not a few flakes, you know. I wanted *plenty* of it! But, boy, it sure worked!" His small chest swelled with pride as he looked out of the hall window at the heavy blanket on the ground.

Molly cleared her throat. "I'm going out to the kitchen and look at the turkey," she said primly. "I can't waste the whole morning listening to this baby talk!"

"You've let yourself get overexcited about Christmas, Toad," Malcolm soothed him. "Run along outside and play with your nice new sled."

The Toad was turning a hideous blotchy purple. Under his lowering brow his bright little eyes disappeared entirely, like the last patches of clear sky behind a thundercloud. "Okay, you guys!" he roared. "I wasn't going to tell you everything, because I knew you wouldn't like it. But you've made me mad now! Making snow and finding our Christmas tree isn't *all* I've done! You want to know the real reason Miss Eva stays in bed all day? Because I fixed her, that's why!"

"What do you mean 'fixed her'?" demanded Molly uneasily.

"Just go upstairs and look in my closet in the box marked 'Alphabet Blocks' and you'll see if I can do magic or not! You dumbheads!" The Toad snatched up his new sled, pulled open the front door, and went out, slamming it behind him as loudly as he could.

CHAPTER NINETEEN

TANDING IN THE hall, the crash of the door echoing in their heads, Malcolm and Molly blinked at each other. "You don't think it's true, do you?" Malcolm whispered.

"Of course not!" his sensible sister retorted. "There's no such thing as magic!"

"All the same, we'd better see what's in his closet." And so, rather reluctantly, they climbed the stairs, casting an uneasy glance at Miss Eva's door as they passed. It took only a moment to find the box marked "Alphabet Blocks" on the shelf of the Toad's closet. Malcolm removed the cover, and inside, just as the Toad had said, lay a crudely printed booklet of spells and charms, instructions and diagrams, for every sort of magic you could think of.

Malcolm leafed through it with a long shudder. "Love potions—finding lost articles—foretelling the future—Oh, Molly, it's true! This proves it!"

"It proves nothing at all," replied his sister curtly, "except that he sent in for a magic kit. It certainly doesn't mean that any of it *works*! Those things on the back of horror comics are fakes and gyps!"

"There's something else in the bottom of the box," Malcolm muttered, drawing out a small knobby package carefully wrapped in newspaper. He had only partly undone it, when sharp-eyed Molly, calm and critical up to now, gave a scream and covered her eyes with her hands.

"Oh, no! *No!* Don't unwrap it!" she begged. "Don't let me look! I know what it is! I've heard of them. They do it in Africa. It's a wax image, and you make it look like your enemy! And then you—then you—oh, Malcolm, are there any pins stuck in it? I can't stand it if there are pins in it. Don't let me see!"

Poor Malcolm was unnerved to see his dependable, matter-of-fact sister go to pieces before his eyes. Nevertheless, with white lips and trembling fingers the courageous oldest Persever unwrapped the sinister package. There was a moment of silence. Then, in a shaken voice, Malcolm reported, "There aren't any pins. But you're right about the rest. It's Miss Eva, all right!"

Molly took her hands away from her face and opened one eye. In the palm of Malcolm's hand lay a little bed made of cardboard and glue. There was a scrap of flannel over it for a blanket. As for the tiny gray wax figure snuggled under the covers, no one could mistake Miss Eva's thin features crayoned on the face. The eyes were sleepy and half closed, the mouth turned up in a contented smile.

Molly gave a sigh of relief. "No pins," she murmured. "She's just drowsy and happy—

exactly the way she's been all these weeks! Well, at least it isn't *black* magic, Malcolm! As long as it doesn't hurt anybody, it's only called white magic!"

But now that the first shock was over, Malcolm's complicated conscience had awakened and set up a clamor in his brain. "Black magic! White magic! What's the difference! This is terrible, Molly! Our own little brother a witch doctor! What a disgrace to the family! What will Dad say? Or Mrs. Coverlet? Or Reverend Forthright? I blame myself, Molly. We should have been looking after him more closely."

"There's no use being dramatic about it," Molly told him. It was very strange about Molly. The minute she knew there were no pins involved, she became her old practical self again. "Why should the grown-ups ever have to know about this? They wouldn't believe it, anyway. All we have to do is burn up the instruction book and the wax, and that's the end of it. He can't possibly do a thing without them."

"You're right. I'll put them in the fireplace this minute!" On his hands and knees in the closet, Malcolm stuffed the booklet and the cardboard bed with its wax occupant into the alphabet box.

"Wait, Malcolm! We can't burn the little figure yet! Whatever happens to *it*, happens to the *real* Miss Eva!"

Malcolm turned pale.

"First we have to warm the wax very gently in our hands till it melts of its own accord and loses its shape. And when it *isn't* Miss Eva anymore, *then* we burn it in the fireplace."

For what seemed an hour they gingerly passed the wax image back and forth, careful not to drop or squeeze it, warming it between their hands, which felt to them as cold as four blocks of ice. When at last the object they held was no longer a figure but only a piece of gray wax, Malcolm crammed it into the box with the pamphlet and the cardboard bed and ran out of his brother's room down the stairs.

"Is the fireplace draft open?" Molly called, a few steps behind him. But she was a second too late. Malcolm had already struck a match to the Christmas wrappings and ribbon which filled the hearth, and it blazed up with a "pow" like a little explosion. Sure enough, the draft was closed! Smoke billowed into the living room. The children watched helplessly. At the same time, to their great relief, they heard a crackle, like bacon frying, which was the ball of gray wax disappearing forever in the flames.

"Open the window! Open the door!" Molly coughed, groping about in the smoke. The fire, which was only paper, died down as quickly as it had begun. But smoke lay everywhere, and ashes kept floating down from the ceiling like black feathers.

All at once a door upstairs opened, and steps were heard running down toward them. "Help! Horrors! Who set the house on fire?" came a shrill, familiar voice.

"Merry Christmas, Miss Eva!" Malcolm

choked, as hospitably as he could.

"We were just burning some wrapping and, uh—a few other things we wanted to get rid of," Molly explained to the agitated figure she could dimly make out in the doorway.

"I see I recovered in the nick of time," said Miss Eva irritably, "before you children burned the house down."

"Come in, Miss Eva, and sit down!" Malcolm gulped. His eyes were watering from the smoke. "Molly and I were—were just expecting you."

CHAPTER TWENTY

I N HER WOOLLY bathrobe, slippers slapping, Miss Eva darted this way and that, exclaiming, "Phew!" and "Mercy," opening doors and windows, fanning the smoky air with her hands, and finally trotting off toward the kitchen to see "what state *that* was in."

Malcolm and Molly followed her with their eyes, saying nothing. So many unlikely things had happened in the short time since they had opened the Toad's secret box that they could not altogether take them in. And while they were standing in the living room looking dazed, the Toad stamped in the front door and beamed at them from the hall, covered with snow, puffing, and obviously pleased with life, with Christmas, with the snow, and particularly with himself. But the grin froze on his face as he noted the looks of pure horror with which his brother and sister were regarding him.

"We found what you had up there," Malcolm announced grimly.

The Toad shrugged. "So what? It isn't hurting her any. She's perfectly happy in bed. Happier than she ever was before."

"Happy has nothing to do with it!" thundered Malcolm, the boy with the conscience. "It's a question of right and wrong! Magic is wrong! Bad! Wicked!"

"And don't think you're ever going to see any of your horrible witchcraft equipment again!" Molly pointed out with satisfaction. "We got rid of every bit!"

The Toad looked genuinely alarmed. "I hope you were careful how you did it," he muttered, looking apprehensively up the front stairs, in the direction of Miss Eva's bedroom. "You might really hurt somebody!"

"Don't worry!" Molly assured him. "We're not idiots! We melted that—that wax thing very gently, and then we burned everything in the fireplace!"

A voice from the kitchen cried, "Malcolm! Molly! What is the meaning of *this*? Come here this instant."

The Toad's eyes narrowed and he glared at his brother and sister. "So she's down already! If you guys had to ruin my spell, why couldn't you at least wait till we'd had Christmas in peace?"

The three of them filed silently into the kitchen. Miss Eva did not look up at them. She was bending over the half-cooked turkey, which she had smelled roasting and had pulled out of the oven to investigate. "Did Mr. Romaine sell you this miserable creature for a Christmas turkey?" she demanded. "Why, there's hardly any meat on the bones. The legs are picked clean, and the breast looks as if it had been mauled! I shall speak to that man about this, believe me!"

"Don't blame Mr. Romaine," Malcolm begged her. "It was a lovely turkey to start with. It's just that the cats found it last night and nibbled—"

"Cats!" cried Miss Eva Penalty. "And you were going to eat it? Praise Heaven I came downstairs in time to prevent that!"

"But, Miss Eva, we washed it!" Molly assured her.

"With *soap*!" added the Toad, making a face as he uttered the hateful word.

"Oh, there you are, Theobold," said Miss Eva, noticing the Toad for the first time. "Take off those snowy things at once, before you catch pneumonia! Now stand out of my way, children! Human beings never eat things which have been mouthed by animals!" She picked up the turkey by its scrawny legs, and marched it out to the little shed off the kitchen. "I'll just wrap it in newspaper and leave it here till we have a path shoveled to the garbage cans," they heard her say.

"I hope you guys are satisfied now!" hissed the Toad under his breath.

"Never mind," Malcolm said with a brave smile. He was determined Christmas was not to be spoiled, and he did not like the look on his little brother's face which was growing fiercer and blacker every minute, the way it always did just before the Toad said or did something ghastly. "Never mind, everybody. We still have the sweet potatoes and the ice cream we bought. And Mr. Forthright's bringing a ham and Mr. Bouncer's coming with plum pudding and brandy."

"Brandy?" Miss Eva squealed, so shocked that her eyelids blinked as rapidly as airplane propellers. "I assure you there will be no alcohol served at the table while *I* am here!"

"But you *have* to put brandy on plum pudding to make it flame!" Molly protested. "Plum pudding by itself is nothing but old dry brown cake stuffed with queer fruit you never heard of!"

"If you feel that way about it, Molly, you needn't eat any!" sniffed Miss Eva. "Plum pudding is highly indigestible for children, anyway."

Malcolm was in despair. "Without a turkey, and without plum pudding, what kind of Christmas will we have *left*?"

"My dear children!" said Miss Eva, "I am not trying to be unkind. Your father himself wanted you to wait to celebrate Christmas until he and Mrs. Coverlet were back. Instead of which, in your headstrong way, you've gone ahead on your own and taken on more than you could manage. You've only yourselves to blame!"

The Toad suddenly began to hop up and down in one spot with his fists clenched. *"Today is Christmas!"* he bellowed. "And we were doing just fine till—"

"Quiet, Toad!" Molly said sharply.

"If I only still had my witchcraft kit!" roared the infuriated boy, "I'd put you under such a spell that—rr-m-n—" Malcolm got his hand over his little brother's mouth in the nick of time. Miss Eva, who had not understood a word the Toad was talking about, blinked at him in bewilderment. At that instant, to everybody's relief, they heard the front door open and Mr. Forthright's cheery voice.

"Merry Christmas, everyone! All right if I let myself in? What a snow! Where is everybody?"

"In the kitchen, Mr. Forthright!" Molly called weakly.

Miss Eva clutched her bathrobe, muttered, "Gracious, I'm not *dressed*!" and scurried up the back stairs to her room.

"Yum, yum! Smell the turkey!" said Mr. Forthright, poking his pleasant face in through the swinging door from the dining room. (The air in the kitchen was still fragrant from the warm drippings in the empty turkey pan.) "Here's my contribution to the feast. Not a big ham, but we'll each get a sliver if you have a good sharp knife." He set a round platter on the kitchen table. The children's hearts sank. It was a pretty enough ham that lay before them, glazed with brown sugar and yellow circles of pineapple. It was as sweet and succulent and willing a little ham as you could ask for. You felt at once that it would do its best for you. But, oh dear, it was just not big enough for six!

Mr. Forthright was so full of talk about the snowstorm that he did not notice the gloomy atmosphere in the Persevers' kitchen. "Amazing blizzard!" he chatted. "Unheard of for these parts! The phone lines are down. Loganbury is completely cut off from the world. Goodness, I forgot to ask about Miss Penalty! Better, you say, and getting dressed to come down? Good! About this snow, though—I called it white magic in my sermon this morning, and there *is* something uncanny about it." (Malcolm and Molly looked at each other unhappily.) "Two or three miles out of town they didn't get a flake. Not a flake! Mr. Bovine was telling me after the service. He has a dairy farm, west of Loganbury. Didn't have any idea there'd been snow till he reached the outskirts of town. He couldn't have made it to church if he hadn't been right behind a snowplow."

The doorbell rang again. "That'll be Mr. Bouncer," said Molly, running to see. Sure enough, there stood their father's jovial boss, puffing and panting, stamping snow off his boots. His face was brighter than a fire engine, and crinkled in a smile. In one hand he was holding a silver plate with a plum pudding. In the other was a bottle of brandy.

"Take these, my dear," he said to Molly, "while I leave my galoshes out here."

A minute later he and Molly had joined the others in the kitchen. "Merry Christmas, all!" Mr. Bouncer beamed. "Oh, Reverend Forthright! Delightful sermon this morning! I liked your calling the snow 'white magic.' Very inspirational thought! Now I'll just set this pudding down here beside the ham. I'm going to pour brandy over it. Watch this, kids! Here's the secret of a good flaming pudding. You've got to let it soak up, you see. Otherwise—"

"Stop, Mr. Bouncer!" Pale but unflinching, honest Malcolm stepped forward and laid a restraining hand on Mr. Bouncer's arm. "We can't—you mustn't—Miss Penalty says—" and the noble boy blurted out not only Miss Eva's harsh decree about the plum pudding, but, while he was at it, the sad fate of their Christmas turkey. "So you see," he concluded, looking miserably at the floor, "after we invited you to Christmas dinner, we have nothing to give you but potatoes and ice cream."

"And olives and cranberry sauce," added Molly, who liked to be literal.

A shadow of disappointment crossed Mr. Bouncer's round face, for he was a hearty man who loved to eat, and he had been licking his chops all morning whenever he thought about Christmas dinner. Still, he said gallantly, "Never mind. We all stuff ourselves too much over the holidays. Do us good to go lightly for a change."

But the small Toad, glowering in a corner, was not to be reconciled. "Everything was going fine until Miss Eva came down!" he growled, adding with an accusing look at his brother and sister, "if *some people* had only left well enough alone—"

"Now, Theobold," Mr. Forthright reproved him, "you must understand that Miss Eva is responsible for you, and unfortunately, grown-ups sometimes have to make decisions which children don't li—"

"Not even a grown-up has a right to spoil Christmas!" proclaimed the unrepentant child, looking Reverend Forthright straight in the eye.

At this uncomfortable moment, Miss Eva herself, in her best dress, came tripping into the kitchen, all smiles. "Reverend! Mr. Bouncer!" she exclaimed. "How kind of you to come! I'm afraid we haven't much of a feast to offer you two hungry men, but I've been laid up in bed till this very morning."

"I must say the rest has done you good, Miss Eva," said Mr. Forthright, cordially taking her hand. "I've never seen you look so blooming."

Miss Eva blushed. "I'll admit I seem to have put on several pounds. I had quite a time just now getting into my good dress. Let's go into the dining room, shall we? And, Reverend, I'm sure our humble meal will seem more generous if you'll oblige us first with a Christmas blessing."

Mr. Forthright took his place at the head of the table. When he had said grace, he picked up the carving knife and gazed down at his meek little ham. Would it go round? Once again his lips moved, this time in silent prayer. Every eye was on his hand as he began to slice; every hand clasped its mate out of sight beneath the tablecloth. Everyone's attention was so riveted upon Mr. Forthright's endeavor that they all gave a start when there was a stamping and scraping of feet on the porch outside, the front door burst open, and footsteps came running through the house. Around the corner into the dining room sailed a plump, stylish person in a fur coat and dazzling hat made of red velvet, whom the children took for a stranger till she reached out her arm and cried, "Darlin's! Darlin's! Have you not a word of greeting for me?" and under the hat they recognized the dear old face of Mrs. Coverlet.

Then up jumped the three Persevers from the table, and somehow Mrs. Coverlet managed to squeeze and be squeezed by all of them at once. Meanwhile, over the children's, heads she smiled at the astonished grown-ups still sitting at the table, until her eyes took in the empty plates, the modest dish of potatoes, the scrap of a ham, and her smile collapsed. "Oh, I'm too late!" she wailed. "You've eaten already! My heart is broken, for I've driven clear down from New York with such a *'uge* turkey as you'd never believe! And such grand fixings to go with it! Such gravy! Such mince and pecan and pumpkin pies as I've gone and baked! And all for nothing! For I see you've eaten everything on the table, and the last thing you want is a Christmas feast!"

CHAPTER TWENTY-ONE

ON'T CRY, MRS. Coverlet! It isn't the way you think!" beseeched Molly, taking one of their house keeper's limp hands.

"We aren't full of dinner! We've barely started!" Malcolm assured her.

"There wasn't anything to eat anyway," said the Toad.

Mr. Forthright pushed back his chair. "I believe there's someone else at the door," he said.

"Mercy! Of course there is!" cried Mrs. Coverlet. "Mrs. Dextrose-Chesapeake and her chauffeur, Wheeler. They drove me from New York. I was so wild to see the children, I ran up the walk ahead of them!" Sure enough, waiting on the front porch with a pumpkin pie in one hand and a mince pie in the other stood Mrs. Dextrose-Chesapeake, the marvelous lady from New York, who was very rich, loved cats, and was the Toad's particular friend. Just behind her, in his uniform and cap, was Wheeler, holding an enormous, covered roasting pan.

"Wow!" shouted the Toad, his beady eyes lighting up. "Bring the pies and turkey right in!"

"Now, I'm ashamed of you, Theobold!" Mrs. Coverlet scolded him. "Where are your manners? Can't you greet Mrs. Dextrose-Chesapeake when she's come all this way?"

Mrs. Dextrose-Chesapeake stepped inside, smiling. "First things first," she told Mrs. Coverlet calmly. "Plenty of time for talk later. I agree with the Toad. Let's get the food inside and our boots off!"

Then followed ten minutes of milling about and confusion. But somehow or other during the course of it the grown-ups who did not know each other were introduced and wished each other Merry Christmas; Wheeler and Mr. Forthright made several trips up the snowy walk with dishes from the car; Mr. Bouncer and Miss Eva added another leaf to the table and set three more places; Mrs. Coverlet took off her beautiful, first-prize mink coat and her red velvet hat, tied on an apron, and reheated the gravy on the stove; and Mrs. Dextrose-Chesapeake, laying aside her long gloves, sat down composedly on the sofa, with the Persevers on all sides, and explained just exactly how she and Mrs. Coverlet had discovered each other in New York and driven down to Loganbury with a Christmas dinner.

"It was yesterday morning," she began. "I was doing a little last-minute Christmas Eve shopping, and Wheeler had just left me in front of one of the big department stores. As I got off the elevator at the housewares floor, there was quite a crowd gathered. Someone said they were interviewing the lady who had won first prize in the White Blizzard Flour Contest."

"And you recognized Mrs. Coverlet!" Molly exclaimed.

"No, my dear. Remember I'd never met her. She was away last summer, looking after her sick daughter, when I got to know you children. But I went over to watch for a moment, and I heard the man who was interviewing her say that he supposed that winning first prize, including all that money, the fur coat, the trip to New York, must seem like the Christmas wishes of a lifetime come true. Then the lady smiled—rather sadly it seemed to me—and agreed that it had all been wonderful and exciting, and a nest egg for her old age, but if he really wanted to know what her Christmas wish was, it was to be home in Loganbury, cooking a turkey for her three dear charges, Malcolm and Molly and little Theobold.

"Well, you can imagine how I jumped to hear these names! Loganbury? I thought, Malcolm? Molly? And Theobold? Why, this must be Mrs. Coverlet! The Toad's Mrs. Coverlet! And why should she have to be standing on a silly platform in a store at Christmastime if she wants to be home! So I pushed my way out of the crowd, got into the elevator, went down to the ground floor, and had Wheeler drive me as fast as he could to the main offices of the White Blizzard Flour Company. Fortunately, the president is an old, old friend of mine. I marched straight into his office, and I said, 'See here, Doughy! What on earth do you mean by keeping this dear lady, Mrs. Coverlet, on a publicity tour at Christmastime? It's outrageous! How on earth will her family manage without her tomorrow?' Well, Doughy Miller isn't a bad fellow, really. He looked horrified, and said he'd never thought about that, and he certainly didn't want to be unkind to anyone. He agreed that Mrs. Coverlet could go home to Loganbury, and come back and finish the tour any time which was convenient.

"So Wheeler and I rushed off to Mrs. Coverlet's hotel to tell her the good news."

"And did she know *you*?" Malcolm asked.

"As soon as I said I was the Toad's cat lady she did," Mrs. Dextrose-Chesapeake replied. "Well, there was not a moment to be lost if we were going to buy the things we needed for a Christmas dinner and get it ready. Such an afternoon the three of us put in! Thank heavens for Wheeler! From one end of town to the other we went, looking for the fattest turkey we could lay our hands on. And tiny pearl onions to cream. And pecans for pie. And chestnuts for stuffing. And real mincemeat. And fresh squash. Then back to my house, where all three of us rolled up our sleeves. Mrs. Coverlet directed, and Wheeler and I scraped and sliced and did as we were told. It was late in the evening before we were through. Then I suddenly remembered we hadn't called you to say we were coming. So I rang long-distance only to find there was a ter-rific snowstorm in Loganbury and the lines were down. Don't think that discouraged us, though. Not after all our work. We knew Wheeler could get us through. So off we went to bed, and started out today with the feast all cooked. And here we are!"

Mrs. Coverlet appeared in the doorway. "Dinner's ready," she triumphantly announced.

Mrs. Dextrose-Chesapeake took her place at one end of the table, Mr. Forthright at the other. Mr. Bouncer sat on Mrs. Dextrose-Chesapeake's right, and the Toad on her left. Miss Eva and Mrs. Coverlet sat on either side of Mr. Forthright. Malcolm and Molly and Wheeler took the chairs in between. Then how they all ate! And talked. And laughed. And ate some more.

After the plates were cleared, Mrs. Coverlet brought in the pies; one mince, one pumpkin, and one pecan. Everybody was so busy watching her slice them and telling her what kind they wanted—the Toad wanted all three, of course—that nobody noticed Mr.

Bouncer slip out of his chair and tiptoe into the kitchen.

All at once, there he stood in the doorway, victoriously holding a flaming plum pudding before him, with his face, above it, glowing as bright as the pudding. The three Persevers gave cheers of delight, and Miss Eva turned very grim. But before she could utter a sound, Mrs. Dextrose-Chesapeake had exclaimed, "Beautiful! Beautiful! Look, everyone!"

And Mrs. Coverlet, glancing up from the pecan pie, dropped her knife, clasped her hands, and cried, "Plum puddin'! God bless you for thinking of it, Mr. Bouncer! I clean forgot. And the children's dear father always says, 'Christmas dinner isn't Christmas without a flamin' puddin' to top it off.'"

CHAPTER TWENTY-TWO

HEN THE CHRISTMAS feast was over, the Persevers and their friends pushed back their chairs and stood up to stretch. Mrs. Dextrose-Chesapeake, Mr. Forthright, Mr. Bouncer, and the children went into the living room. Miss Eva and Mrs. Coverlet stayed behind to collect the dishes and clear them away. And Wheeler went outdoors to shovel snow off the steps and walks.

No sooner did Mr. Bouncer sit down in a really comfortable chair by the fire than his head began to buzz and he could not keep from yawning. He had eaten a great deal and longed to stretch out and snooze. At last he could bear it no longer, got heavily to his feet, and said he must be getting home. At that Mr. Forthright looked at his watch, saw that it was close to five, and remembered that he had three or four parish calls to make before the day's end.

"I'd like to walk a little way with you, Mr. Forthright," said Malcolm solemnly.

When Mr. Bouncer had gone, and Mr. Forthright had stepped out to the kitchen to say good-bye to Mrs. Coverlet and Miss Penalty, Malcolm went to the hall closet to put on his jacket. His sister Molly followed him.

"I know why you want to go along with Mr. Forthright," she informed him, "and you're a fool if you tell him a word about it!"

"A word about what?" asked Malcolm, defensively.

"Why, Malcolm, I can read you like a book! Your conscience is bothering you about the Toad and that witchcraft nonsense!"

"Nonsense you call it!" Malcolm stared at her incredulously. "You saw what he had up there in his closet! You know the things he made happen! I can't just forget the whole thing!"

"Well, I can!" declared Molly. "And you would too, if you had any sense! After all, there's no harm done. We've burned the stuff, so nothing more can happen. It's been a beautiful Christmas. Why spoil it? You'll only upset Mr. Forthright, and he won't understand a word you say. Matter of fact, Malcolm, I think you and I—well, I think we lost our heads when we found that wax thing. It *was* scary! But it still didn't prove anything. All the things that happened—Miss Eva, the tree, the snow—they all might have been going to happen anyway, in a perfectly normal way!"

"Normal!" snorted Malcolm. "Three feet of snow falling just within the city limits of Loganbury, and no place else in the whole state! Normal!"

Molly shrugged. "Weather's always doing funny things, Malcolm. Next Christmas we might have a heat wave. Take my advice! Don't say anything to Mr. Forthright. Grown-ups don't believe in magic. And for that matter," she added, tilting her chin, and looking him in the eye, "neither do I."

"There you are, my boy!" said Mr. Forthright, appearing in the living room door. "Let's be off!"

Molly watched them from the hall window as they thrust their hands into their coat pockets and went down the porch steps into the chilly twilight. It was lovely and warm in the house and smelled of the Christmas tree. Poor Malcolm's face looked pinched and cold. She was glad she had not been born with a complicated conscience. One was enough for any family.

Malcolm and Mr. Forthright proceeded along Wheeler's freshly cleared walk. The sun had gone down, and the sky was rust-colored. Mr. Forthright drew a deep breath and blew out a cloud of steam. "Beautiful evening! Beautiful snow! And to think of its happening for Christmas! Out of thin air! Like magic!"

"Oh, sir!" groaned Malcolm, "don't say that!"

Mr. Forthright glanced questioningly at his young friend.

"This snow," blurted Malcolm, looking painfully at it piled all around, "it isn't *real*! Oh, I suppose it's real *snow*, all right! But it isn't *natural*!"

Mr. Forthright bent down and scooped up a handful. "It seems perfectly natural to me. Pick it up yourself. Light and powdery, yet it will make a firm ball, too. I'd say it was some of the finest snow I'd ever seen."

"It shouldn't be here—that's the thing!"

"Why, Malcolm! What could be more appropriate for Christmas than snow?"

"Mr. Forthright, I'm going to tell you everything!" Malcolm looked straight up into his friend's eyes. "The Toad made it snow! He's a— or, I should say he *was*—a witch doctor!" The rust-colored sky darkened. The streetlights all went on, like eyes opened in consternation.

"The Toad has been telling us for weeks it was going to snow for Christmas. We didn't believe him, of course. But he'd secretly been casting weather spells all the time, and sure enough, they worked!"

Mr. Forthright cleared his throat. "How on earth did your little brother learn to be a witch doctor here in Loganbury?"

"He sent in for a magic kit on the back of a horror comic!"

"Horror comic?" For the first time Mr. Forthright sounded aghast. "I thought your father had forbidden you to buy them."

"The Toad found this one in an alley. He says he didn't read it. Just looked at the ads on the back. But that was enough!" Malcolm said bitterly.

"I'll have to confess I'm curious about just what comes in a witchcraft kit," murmured Mr. Forthright as they proceeded along the sidewalk.

"Instructions mostly. Directions for weather

brewing—how to make potions—finding things with a willow wand." Malcolm sighed. "I might as well tell you that's the way we got our Christmas tree. And to think I chopped it down myself, never suspecting a thing!"

"You don't mean the beautiful spruce in the living room?"

Malcolm nodded wretchedly.

"But Mr. Bouncer was telling me all about that tree at dinner. He certainly didn't mention any magic. Something about catching you three, red-handed, on his property with it. I must say," observed Mr. Forthright, "none of the Toad's—er—witchcraft sounds too serious to me. In fact, I'm not entirely convinced that any of it was really magic."

"Oh, if only the snow and the tree were *all*," Malcolm broke in, "I could drop the whole thing. But there is something else. Something horrible!"

"Good heavens, old chap! What's that?"

"It's Miss Eva, sir. You know how the Toad

feels about her! When he first learned that she was moving in to look after us, he started to run away to New York to stay with Mrs. Dextrose-Chesapeake. Only Molly and I caught up with him and made him promise to stick it out with us at home." Malcolm groaned. "Maybe we should have let him go! Anyhow, the first night Miss Eva was here it was pretty bad. She made the Toad wash with soap before dinner. Ears and everything. Then, when we ate, it was vegetables, vegetables, and nothing afterwards you could really call dessert. And when she put him to bed, she took all his cats out of his room—you know how he loves them—and shut them in the cellar. I guess that was the last straw." Malcolm shuddered. "Anyway" (cold as the evening was, he felt perspiration break out on his forehead), "anyway, next morning Miss Eva wasn't able to come down to breakfast."

"I've heard all about that, Malcolm," Mr. Forthright assured him. "The strain of looking after you three was apparently too much for her, and she was nervously exhausted."

"That's what Dr. Gargle says, but it's not it, at *all*! The real thing was that the Toad had fixed her so she *couldn't leave her room!*"

"You mean he locked her in?"

"No, sir! Nothing like that." Malcolm took a deep breath and blurted out the terrible facts about the wax image. "Molly and I only found it this morning. The Toad was so pleased with himself about the way the snow had come and everything that he couldn't resist bragging to us. So of course we ran right upstairs to his closet, where he said everything was, and it was all there!"

"What does your practical sister think of all this?" Mr. Forthright inquired.

Malcolm shrugged and sighed. "She was pretty upset at the time, but now that it's all over she claims she still doesn't believe in magic."

"But you do?"

"What else *is* there to believe? Five minutes

after we melted that wax doll, Miss Eva came running downstairs in her bathrobe and slippers—her old self again!"

Mr. Forthright stopped walking. They had reached the hedge outside the Billiards' house, where the minister had promised to drop in. "Not quite her old self again," he said thoughtfully. "I sat next to her at dinner, you know, and noticed a change. She's plumper, and she has a wonderful appetite. She mentioned how much she'd gotten to like hot dogs and hamburgers since you children have been bringing up her trays. And she spoke about all the reading she's done. She told me she's going to spend less time scrubbing woodwork and chasing dogs out of her yard and more time enjoying life. Oh, there's been a change in her, all right. Not a big one, I suppose, but it's for the better." He turned to leave Malcolm. "There's been magic around us, all right," he said. "I felt it very strongly when I came to your house last night and saw you and Molly filling the stockings."

"Then you *do* believe me!"

"I believe in magic at Christmas," said Mr. Forthright reflectively. "The amount of good-will which is set loose every year at this time is quite unaccountable. Take your spruce!" he said suddenly. "I don't care *how* the Toad found it! What good were his spells and his wand if Mr. Bouncer hadn't let you keep it, and even helped you home with it! And what about Mrs. Dextrose-Chesapeake and Mrs. Coverlet? Wasn't their finding each other and coming here almost a miracle? Let the Toad think he conjured up Christmas single-handed. You and I know how many people contributed."

"There was your ham," Malcolm said politely.

Mr. Forthright laughed. "It would have taken some powerful magic to make *that* go around the table, I'm afraid!"

"And there was Mr. Bouncer's flaming pudding!"

"You're forgetting the main thing, Malcolm."

"We already mentioned Mrs. Coverlet's and Mrs. Dextrose-Chesapeake's dinner."

"I mean you and Molly making Christmas in your house for your little brother. Everything else that happened, and everybody else who came along, just fitted in." Mr. Forthright turned in at the Billiards' gate. "It's been a wonderful Christmas, Malcolm. Be easy in your mind. Enjoy it. Enjoy its mysteriousness. Enjoy it all."

The oldest Persever retraced his steps to his house. Over his head hung the swinging stars, and between him and them were the black nets of winter branches. Molly was right. There was no use discussing witchcraft with the Reverend Forthright. Grown-ups simply don't believe in magic. And yet he was glad he had talked to Mr. Forthright. Even if his friend knew nothing about witchcraft, he understood a good deal about Christmas.

As he came up the walk to his house he heard the front door open and saw Miss Eva come down the porch steps in her coat and hat, with Wheeler following with her suitcase.

"I wish you wouldn't leave us so soon," Mrs. Coverlet's voice was saying. "I'm about to make turkey sandwiches and cocoa."

"Don't tempt me, my dear! I'm terribly anxious to get home," replied Miss Eva.

"Good night, Miss Eva, and thanks a lot for staying with us," Molly called from the door politely.

"Yeah—thanks!" came the Toad's voice, strangely thick and forced. "And quit twisting my ear, Molly!"

By stepping off the path behind a bush, Malcolm let Miss Eva and Wheeler pass without seeing him. He was in such a privately peaceful state of mind that he hated to spoil it by talking to anyone. There was no one in sight as he slipped in the front door, but he could hear Mrs. Coverlet, Mrs. Dextrose-Chesapeake, and Molly in the living room. It seemed to him that a piece of cold pecan pie would go nicely just then, so he started along the back hall toward the kitchen. As he reached the doorway he heard the rustle of newspaper and, looking in, saw that his little brother had retrieved the poor, chewed turkey Miss Eva had discarded on the back porch, brought it inside and was proudly unwrapping it on the kitchen table.

"Here you are, cats!" the Toad was saying in a kingly tone as he sat down in a kitchen chair. Out from under the table came Heather, Mary Mouse, George Soup, Ernest Waffle, Sally Egg, and John Napkin and sat before him in a row on the kitchen floor.

"Here's a turkey just for you!" said the Toad. "I know you already started it last night, but you'll like it better now that it's cooked." He began to pull off bite-sized morsels to distribute. But he had scarcely started when John Napkin jumped into his lap and took hold of the biggest piece in his little teeth. "Down, bad boy!" commanded his master. "Don't be a greedy! There's plenty for all. Here's the first piece for you, Heather, because you're the mother. Now George. Here, Mary Mouse, don't be shy. It's *Christmas*! The best day in the year. Listen, I'm going to tell you something," he said confidentially to the six upturned faces. "With Dad and Mrs. Coverlet away, I wasn't sure how Christmas would turn out. Of course, Santa Claus saw to the presents. I didn't have to worry about *those*. But all the rest, I took care of myself, with magic. You see, I'm the smart one in the family," he explained with satisfaction. "Malcolm and Molly couldn't manage anything without me."

In the back hall, unseen, Malcolm put his hand over his mouth and smiled. But the six cats, sitting in a respectful row, looked up at their master and believed every word he said.